George Dunn

Red Cap and Blue Jacket

Vol. 1

George Dunn

Red Cap and Blue Jacket
Vol. 1

ISBN/EAN: 9783337329556

Printed in Europe, USA, Canada, Australia, Japan

Cover: Foto ©Andreas Hilbeck / pixelio.de

More available books at **www.hansebooks.com**

RED CAP AND BLUE JACKET

BY

GEORGE DUNN

'Αλλὰ παλαιὰ γὰρ
εὔδει χάρις, ἀμνάμονες δὲ βροτοί

IN THREE VOLUMES

VOL. I.

WILLIAM BLACKWOOD AND SONS
EDINBURGH AND LONDON
MDCCCXCIV

CONTENTS OF THE FIRST VOLUME.

RED CAP AND BLUE JACKET.

PROLOGUE.

ANNO DOMINI 1781, the 25th day of January. It is a coral islet in the South Pacific, a circular ridge of rock enclosing a tranquil lagoon, the bosom of which heaves with a languid rhythm responsive to the long swell of billows which break in monotonous thunder on the shore, and crowd a mass of water into the narrow opening which connects the lagoon with the boundless waste of ocean. The rock is clothed with luxuriant vegetation, and groves of palms wave their feathery foliage in the breeze. On the southern segment of the belt of coral the

disintegration of the calcareous substance of
the rock has formed a tiny beach white as
snow and glancing with dazzling brightness
in the sunshine.   Here the mutilated skeleton of a ship lies high and dry.   A rude hut,
constructed of planking and *débris* of the
wreck, and thatched with palm-fronds, stands
near the edge of the lagoon in a spot shel-
tered from the prevailing winds.   On the
highest summit of the rock appears one of
the ship's spars with a pennant fluttering at
the top.

On the afternoon of this 25th day of
January a man was standing beside this
improvised flag-staff or signalling-station,
and sweeping the horizon with a telescope.
His motionless and statuesque attitude bespoke the calm endurance of one habituated
to stoical passivity by repeated disappoint-
ments.   His tattered and faded habiliments
still bore traces of having been the uniform
of a naval officer.   A sword hung by his
side.   Another man — for he had a companion — was lying prone on the ground
beside the hut, and gazing with the same

motionless intensity into the pellucid waters of the lagoon.

This natural aquarium presented indeed a lovely sight. The sea-flags were swaying gracefully to and fro, long strips of crimson dulse undulated with the movement of the water, the coral-tree dipped its green leaves and bunches of scarlet blossoms into the water with every gust of wind, while purple mullets and goldfish were darting with incessant and capricious motion through the glassy element, and gorgeous sea-anemones flaunted their pink and snowy filaments.

At last the recumbent figure rose with a long-drawn sigh and entered the hut. He put some fresh cocoa-nut husks upon the fire that was smouldering on a slab of rock, and looked into the pot suspended gipsy-fashion over it. As he did so he muttered, as it seemed, unconsciously to himself, like one impelled to self-converse in the dearth of social intercourse. He looked for some time at the sodden mass of kalo-root that had been left to stew slowly, and then, with an abrupt gesture, took out of his pocket a silver whistle, and blew a shrill blast as a signal to his companion. The latter, after a considerable interval, appeared, breathing somewhat quickly, and with a far-away look in his eyes.

"Another of your savoury dishes, Ralph," he said in a harsh tone.

"Another of the same, Nicholas," said his companion. "It doesn't take long to box the compass of our cookery. Yams, kalo-root, cocoa-nut, and their permutations through this eternity of time which mortals call a year."

"We are not sufficiently inventive, methinks. There should be plenty of edible fishes."

"The last we tried nearly poisoned us, if you remember."

"They were too beautiful to be good. 'Tis a natural parable, perchance," rejoined Nicholas, with a mocking ring in his voice.

"Nay, it is the wise parsimony of nature. In these desolate regions there are no mouths to eat wholesome fish."

"Nor eyes to admire their beauty."

"The old controversy, Nicholas," said Ralph with a smile. "Be sure they are beautiful to the great Artist."

"Tush! their brilliant colours are meant to make them attractive to their destroyers. Their beauty is their destruction. Another parable!"

"Attractive to their destroyers? More probably to their mates. A harmless parable this time!"

So saying, he ladled out a quantity of the stringy substance into a cocoanut-shell, handed it to his companion, and then helped himself.

"According to all sound social principles," said Nicholas, with an unpleasant smile, "I ought to do all the cooking, instead of taking it in turn."

"The conventions of society do not exist here," said Ralph. "You and I are now strictly equal in the eye of nature. You might draw a diameter through the island, and insist upon my keeping within my proper limits. I a peer of the realm, forsooth! What realm? Assuredly not that of nature.

I should indeed get a new scutcheon—a row of sweet-potatoes *azure*, a palm-branch *pendant*, a pot *sable*, and so forth. And for the motto or device — what say you? 'Immersabilis undis,' or 'qui meruit *palmam* ferat.'"

"You can still be merry, it appears," said Nicholas.

"Very deadly merriment; much as a prisoner might clank his fetters for amusement."

"I wonder if we shall ever taste again the roast-beef of old England," said Nicholas, after a long silence, and mechanically turning his head round towards the flag-staff.

"Out, mocking fiend!" cried Ralph, melodramatically. "Don't recall the sweet visions of the past which hover through the odorous steams of hospitable inns and cook-shops. Dost remember the George at Dover, Nicholas, and mine host who was a standing certificate of good cheer? I' faith, I understand the nobility of a baron of beef now. I would exchange my patent for one."

"You would think differently if a ship

hove in sight," said Nicholas. Ralph was silent for a few moments, and then said—

"Think you, I care for barren honours, my good cousin? But for my wife and my sweet child——"

He stopped short, shivered spasmodically, while a choking sob rose in his throat, and his eyes filled with sudden tears.

Nicholas knitted his brows, and drummed his fingers nervously on the rough table at which they sat.

"I am thankful I have neither wife nor child to think of," he said.

"Nay, Nicholas, 'tis the thought of my two loved ones that keeps me from absolute despair. I must live, I shall live, and see them again. God in His mercy——"

"Pooh, pooh," exclaimed Nicholas, in a tone of cold contempt; "it is all chance. Think you that *we* are of any consequence in this boundless universe? No, no; I hold with good old Homer: Jove is away from home, dining with the blameless Æthiopians."

"It is a poor creed, Nicholas, and makes poor men; for if we could suppose the

Supreme Being careless of any of His creatures, it would be an argument for human
selfishness.   Why should we not also dine
with the Æthiopians?   Nay, nay; not a
sparrow falls without His permission."

"Why does He let the sparrow fall, then?"
retorted Nicholas, with a gruff laugh.

"Because it is time, my short - sighted
cousin.   Think of the joys a poor sparrow
has—its ecstasy of buoyant flight, its career-
ing freedom — ay, we poor prisoners can
faintly imagine that.   The sparrow has its
day of sunny bliss.   It would be cruel to
condemn it to a helpless, feeble-pinioned age."

Nicholas laughed boisterously.

"'Tis a grotesque idea, enough—a bald,
white-feathered sparrow."

"Yes," continued Ralph, musingly.   "The
atheist thinks like Alphonso of Castile, that
he could have constructed a better world if
he had infinite power; but he is a fool, as
the Psalmist says, and 'tis as impossible for
him to conceive a better scheme of creation
as for the sparrow we speak of to construct
a science of zoology."

" Spoken like a bishop—' in partibus in-
fidelium,' " said Nicholas, scoffingly. " I wish
you joy of your creed. But it is easy to
approve of the dispensations of Providence
when one has a title, a large rent-roll, and
all the pleasures of eye and sense."

Ralph, smiling, made a sweeping movement with his arm.

" Pshaw ! " exclaimed Nicholas, replying
to his cousin's gesture. " We shall not be
always here. At least, I hope I shall not.
Then good-bye to natural equality ! Then
it will be ' Your Lordship,' ' gros comme le
bras.' You are merely a planet in occulta-
tion. You will re-trick your beams."

" You speak as if you grudged me those
accidental advantages," said Ralph, reproachfully. " And yet I have not concentrated
them within myself. I have treated you as
my friend."

" You mean, you have allowed me to be
your parasite," replied Nicholas, with a
lowering brow.

" Nay, do not let us bandy harsh words,"
said Ralph, gently. " I know this pitiless

serenity of nature breeds exasperation; but let us prove that we have the robust virtues of a harsher clime."

" Why, there you are again—my moral as well as my material benefactor. You are a dripping well of philosophic maxims. You thus assert your superiority, and fix me in a low subordination, a humiliating pupilage."

" Grant, nevertheless, that I have never aired superiority," said Ralph, with a pained look.

" I grant it. But observe : your studious and circumspect endeavour to ignore the distinctions of rank, your very affectation of equality, has in it something more keenly galling than the calm or even the blunt assertion of superiority. And you drape yourself with the added virtue of magnanimity."

" That is the language of morbid pride," said Ralph, impatiently. " But I do not wish to quarrel with you. It is a hard thing, I know, for two men to live in such isolation as ours without becoming wearied of one another. The best of us need to be socially diluted. It would have been better for us if we had had to struggle for our subsistence. Life, such as it is, has been too easy. We have not been compelled to work off our spleen. It is significant that man is most ferocious where nature is most benignant. This Pacific Ocean breeds cannibals. Come, Nicholas, let us be reasonable. Do not let us forget that we are still Englishmen."

" 'Tis easy for you to philosophise. The only slave-philosopher was Epictetus, and he taught stoicism. And I am still too young for that. And besides, the passions have their own logic."

He cast down his head with a fierce and brooding look.

"What passions? I do not understand you, Nicholas," said Ralph, coldly.

"Do you forget that you robbed me of the woman I loved?" asked Nicholas, after a long pause.

"Ah! that, then, is the major premiss of your logic of the passions," said Ralph, drawing in his breath, and growing pale.

" Yes, I loved the woman whom you made
your wife because you could not obtain her
on easier terms."

" 'Tis a foul calumny," said Ralph, hotly.

" Foul !—calumny ! You say that to me ?
Take care ! "

" Yes, for I honoured her too highly to
dream of any looser tie than marriage."

" Honoured her ? And yet you concealed
your marriage, as if she had been your
mistress."

" I owe you no account of my actions.
But, as you well know, there were potent
reasons. The aristocratic pride of my father
and mother—as fanatical and irrational as
it was deeply rooted—would have refused
to recognise as my wife one who had been
on the lyric stage. I wished to spare her
humiliation."

" The usual cant ! Whether would she
be more humiliated by the cold disdain of
your bigoted family or by the indignity of
a clandestine marriage ? "

" You are insolent, sir. She understood
me, and was willing to be patient. But

enough, and more than enough, of that. I would have called any other man to account for such language."

Nicholas contemptuously shrugged his shoulders.

"And am I to understand," continued Ralph, with sparkling eyes, " that all this time you have cherished rancour and hatred because *she* preferred me to you? You have been wearing a mask, have you? What a monster of duplicity you make yourself to be !"

"Had not your self-complacency been so great," retorted Nicholas, with a burning brow, "you would easily have detected my feelings. Have I ever made a show of affection? But have it so ! I concealed my plebeian hatred as you concealed your plebeian amours. We have both lived in glass houses——"

"Stained glass !" said Ralph, cuttingly. "But what means this manœuvred outburst? Do you wish to pick a quarrel with me ?"

"You have taken your full share in the

altercation. I, too, would have called any
other man to account for your looks, tones,
and language. If your sword is fretting in
its scabbard, out with it! I care not if
I receive a mortal wound. This is not
life, it is purgatory."

"Because you make it so. Oh God!
has it come to this?" cried Ralph, with
a look and gesture of agonised despair.
"Here are two men separated from all
the kind intercourse of their fellow mortals, sharing the same dangers, privations,
miseries, and yet they must add tenfold
wretchedness to their hapless lot. Oh,
Nicholas, self-pity should make you pitiful.
I do not understand you, I do not recognise you. Is it temporary madness? Are
you running amuck like a wild Malay? I
have often proved your chivalry, your loy-
alty. When the men took to the boats,
you refused to abandon me. There was
the Nicholas I knew. I did not rob you
of *her*. I did not supplant you. You
knew her before me. What of that? Was
she not free to bestow her love? Oh,

Nicholas, be your own true self! I have not so stout a heart as you have. I need a little friendship, a little kind companionship to keep me from madness or absolute despair. Or if this may not be, plunge your sword into my heart and rid me of an intolerable existence."

"It is you who are insane," replied Nicholas, drawing himself up. "Do you take me for an assassin? I would kill myself rather than kill another—save by an honourable duel. You speak of wretchedness. You cannot be as wretched as I am. You have the recollection of *her* love. You have been in paradise. I know only the hell of jealousy and baffled longing."

"Your passion does not carry conviction," said Ralph, with a scrutinising and suspicious glance. "It looks like stagethunder. You have loved many women—and forgotten them! A voluptuary, and yet so tragically constant! You are gilding a baser passion. Is it envy? is it cupidity? is it the sour resentment of a man defrauded by nature and society of his proper place? If so, you are blighting and searing your own heart. You are deepening your own misery. You are digging a grave for every high aspiration, every generous thought. This purgatory that you spoke of will become a hell. How can we live together on such terms? And yet, how forbear to live together? Think of it."

"You are eloquent as usual," said Nicholas, coldly. "I shall not imitate you. It is useless to harangue the passions. No Greek tragedian ever made Chiron lecture Hercules when tortured by the shirt of Nessus. As for living together, how does many a woman live with her husband, hating and scorning him as her legalised tyrant or her brute associate? Enough, and more than enough, as you have said. I leave you for the present."

Ralph watched his cousin hastily return to his post of observation, and then he sadly wended his way to the stretch of level beach near which his ship had struck the outer ring of rock that encircled the island. The battered hulk and giant ribs of the wreck looked like the skeleton of some monstrous saurian belonging to an antediluvian age ; the hawse-holes in the still solid bows simulated empty eye-sockets; and the broken bowsprit a protruding horn —so weird and illusive was the scene in the commingling of day and night. There " at one stride comes the dark " ; and soon the sky was studded with unfamiliar constellations. In his grief and forlornness, Ralph's heart yearned towards the serenity of the illimitable heavens. He fixed his eyes on the Southern Cross, wondering if this group of stars had been set in the skies as a holy symbol. He murmured the sacred words — " Which maketh Arcturus, Orion, and Pleiades, and the chambers of the south," as a kind of answer to his speculative inquiry.

After pacing to and fro for an hour, wrapped in painful musings, he sat down in a hollow of the rock ; and ere long, lulled by the soft whisper of the wind and the voluminous roar of the surf, he fell asleep.

Meanwhile, Nicholas stood beside the flag-staff fiercely and feverishly intent. No, it had not been the white glimmer of a bird's wing or a larger patch of foam. A vessel was rising fast in the offing, and seemed to be heading for the island under a press of canvas. A couple of hours passed, and the outlines of masts, spars, and sails, bathed in the milky light of the rising moon, became defined like some delicate carving in ivory. Only a streak of white under the vessel's bows showed the speed of her approach.

"It is now high time," he muttered, and descended from his post of observation. An hour passed, and then the report of a cannon broke the stillness, and awoke a thousand answering cries of affrighted sea-birds. Shortly after, Nicholas reappeared on the summit of the rock, pale, weary, and haggard. He began to haul the pennant up and down with frantic haste. The vessel —evidently an English frigate—stood about half a mile from the island, hove-to, her fore-sail slowly lifting, her main-topsail

laid aback and fluttering against the mast.
Then a boat was lowered promptly and
pulled towards the island. The feathered
oars, moving like parts of some perfect
machine, glanced in the moonshine. As
the boat came near, Nicholas by shouts
and gestures directed the steersman towards a practicable landing - place. The
boat was run aground, and the young midshipman who had been seated in the stern-
sheets bounded nimbly ashore. He gazed
at Nicholas with curiosity and interest.

"Who are you, sir?" he asked, with precocious dignity.

"A miserable shipwrecked man," said
Nicholas, hoarsely. "Take me off, for
God's sake—I mean——"

"Are you the only man on the island?"
interrupted the youthful officer.

"The only living man. For pity's sake,
take me away from this accursed spot."

"Have you no property or belongings
to remove?"

"Nothing, nothing," cried Nicholas, impatiently stamping his foot.

"You are in a devil of a hurry, it appears," remarked the midshipman. "Any savages about?"

"No,—yes,—some perhaps;" and he passed his hand across his brow.

The young officer glanced round at his crew and significantly tapped his forehead.

"In with you then," he said, in a more subdued tone.

Nicholas sprang into the boat, and sitting down on one of the thwarts, buried his face in his hands.

"Push off, men, and give way," said the midshipman.

CHAPTER I.

A VILLAGE SCHOOL A CENTURY AGO.

IN the same year as that in which our tale
commenced, Andrew Prosser, A.M. of Aber-
deen University, was appointed schoolmaster
of Fownie, a village on the east coast of
Scotland. He was a native of the Mearns,
and had lost both parents when he was a
boy ; but being of "pregnant parts," according to the old-fashioned phrase, he had so
well profited by the drilling in Latin and
Greek which he received at the parish
school that he gained a bursary at Aber-
deen University, and, after a four years'
course, took his degree. He was a youth
of twenty when he came to Fownie, and for
twelve years he had uneventfully discharged

the duties of his office. He was now a tall, stalwart man, with a handsome well-proportioned figure, and in his student days he had been a redoubtable wrestler. Like most very powerful men he was good-natured, and his look of professional austerity hardly imposed upon any one, least of all upon his pupils, who, however, had a salutary respect for his physical prowess. At this time no one spoke of moral suasion — probably the phrase had not been invented — and school discipline was maintained at the point of the tawse. Moral offences, indeed, were treated — as if they had been cutaneous eruptions—by external applications. Andrew's predecessor had been thoroughly imbued with this principle, which might not unaptly be summarised in the satirical lines written by an appreciative schoolboy—

> " *Hic, hæc, hoc,*
> Give the dunce a knock;
> *Amandum, amandi,*
> You're in for a pandy."

Accordingly, Andrew had found the boys

brutalised and the girls morbidly timid;
and since the dominie was regarded as
the natural enemy of boys, much as the
French were considered to be the natural
enemies of the British, Andrew had experienced the playful humour of his pupils in
various ways. Each scholar came to school
in winter with a contributory peat under
his arm; and once or twice a miniature
explosion occurred, a small quantity of pow-
der having been inserted into the heart of
an innocent - looking peat. Occasionally,
also, a pod of cayenne pepper was cunningly
thrown into the fire, with the result that
master and pupil sneezed in unison for a
quarter of an hour to an accompaniment of
stifled bursts of laughter instead of God-
bless - you's. Sometimes, by preconcerted
arrangement, the slate-pencil or "skeely"
of all the youthful arithmeticians began to
make screeching and scraping sounds which
might have corrugated the skin of an alli-
gator. The quart ink-bottle now and then
yielded treacle instead of ink. A blackened
portion of the wall, which served instead of

a black-board, frequently exhibited Andrew's features, in which the slight cast of his left eye was prodigiously exaggerated. To such sketches various festive mottoes were attached, such as "swivels," "gleed - eyed Andy" (in impossible spelling), "hard-a-port," and so forth. Andrew, in those times of probation, would certainly have subscribed very heartily to Plato's statement that a boy is a most plotting and "insidious beast." In process of time, however, his good humour, supported by his vigorous biceps, gained the mastery ; and at the epoch when our narrative opens there was probably not another dominie in the county so much beloved and respected.

The schoolhouse was a two-storeyed building with a thatched roof, the ground-floor being occupied by the schoolroom — there was but one—and the three apartments on the floor above forming Andrew's abode. It stood on the brow of a hill overlooking the sea.

The schoolroom was a moderate - sized apartment, low in the roof, and floored with planks well worn by hundreds of shuffling feet, and studded with defiant knots and knobs, like warts upon a well-shaven countenance. The limited space was lumbered with heavy unwieldy desks, the surface of which was like "the ribbed sea-sand," the more friable fibres of the wood having yielded to the attrition of two or three generations of corduroy cuffs ; while notches, hacks, initials, and arabesques, executed by bold if untutored pocket - knives, formed " woodcuts " little reconcilable with the canons of art.

The master's desk, a massive and monumental structure, resembling a pulpit shorn of its base (which is an allegory importing the relation of the schoolmaster to the minister), stood near the huge open fireplace. In those days there were no grates skilfully contrived for conveying the heat up the chimney. A map of Europe, with its lower edge tattered and fringed, hung upon the wall, pale and ghostly, its original colours having faded to a nondescript hue. A pointer leaned against a corner of the room, its taper end charred to a blackened stump, it being a handy implement, useful for poking either the fire or the ribs of lounging and lethargic pupils.   In another corner stood a terrestrial globe, which had been baptised with a bottle of ink, and now represented nothing but primeval chaos, out of which the British Isles dimly emerged, with a segment of the hostile shore of France. In another dark corner lay a smooth flat stone, on which misdemeanants in former days had been set to cool after castigation —a delicate antiphlogistic attention.

It was not yet eight o'clock, for in summer the school opened at seven. A class of twelve, boys and girls intermixed, was floundering through the proper names in a chapter of Nehemiah; while Andrew was pointing and trimming the quills for future use, occasionally interjecting a mild and expostulatory correction.

"John Dempster, look at the word. It isna Cherub-babble, it's Zerubbabel. Ye needna misca' the puir man. He's dead now, and 'de mortuis nil nisi bonum'—what does that mean, Sandy?"

" Please, sir, I dinna ken," said Sandy.

" You should put a wee bit label on your skull, Sandy, ' To let, unfurnished.'   That's the broad phylactery that would suit *you.* Ye're a minus quantity, ay, and an irrational quantity forby.   Next boy ! "

" ' The children of Hashum,' " went on the " next boy " in a dull level voice, " ' three hundred twenty and eight.' "

" Ay, ay," remarked Andrew, sarcastically, " I haena got sae mony o' the children o' *Hash'em,* but I've got ower mony for a' that."

And on the chapter went till it closed with the welcome remark—" ' When the seventh month came, the children of Israel were in their ceeties.' "

" Ay, ay, that's fine reading ; ye can gang to *your seaties,*" was Andrew's dry comment. " Latin class come forward.   John Dempster's class, take your grammar and parse the words in Exercise 24.   And next time, John, that ye're parsing ' in the times of Abraham,' dinna say that ' times ' is in the objective case governed by *Abraham.*   Dinna mix up grammatical and patriarchal government, there's a braw lad !"

John, a logger-headed urchin with a very tousled head, shambled to his seat, followed by the rest of his class-mates.

The Latin class consisted of three, two boys and a girl. Andrew took his seat on his three-legged stool, and glanced round upon the three with a genial smile, which the two lads sheepishly returned. The girl, meanwhile, with a calm and earnest countenance was turning up the place. She was dressed in a somewhat faded but spotlessly clean print frock ; and, while most of the girls had their feet encased in large and clumsy shoes, — some of them evidently derelict and secured as salvage, — she wore small and dainty shoes with steel buckles. Her hands, though somewhat coarsened with manual labour, were small, white, and finely formed. She was indeed a charming maiden, all the more so that she was utterly uncon-scious of her attractions. The face was purely and delicately moulded, the eyebrows were chastely arched above deep - blue thoughtful eyes, the small mouth wore an expression of mingled sadness and sweetness ; and when she smiled — which was seldom — she showed regular teeth white as milk.   Her form was slight and girlish, but justly proportioned, and gave promise of maidenly grace and symmetry.   But perhaps her greatest charm was her voice, which was exquisitely soft and rich, full of caressing modulations and delicate surprises of tone, so that when she spoke— and she was chary of speech—her simplest utterances haunted the ear with undefined delight, and she might have talked nonsense with impunity.   When she began to translate, the scratching quills and scraping pencils stopped, and the boys and girls in the desks forgot their tasks to gaze and listen with open mouths and ears.   On the present occasion they experienced a new sensation—they heard her laugh ; and broad uncomprehending grins overspread every face, so magical and so musical was the sound.   Her laugh — whereat she instantly blushed a dark crimson — was caused by a mistranslation perpetrated by one of her companions, Thomas Fairley, a flaxen-headed, amiably stupid lad, designed by his parents for the ministry. This youth, on coming to the line—

"Infandum, regina, jubes renovare dolorem,"
Thou bidst me, queen, renew unutterable woe—

rendered it thus unhappily — "the queen bids her infant renew its grief."

Andrew was too much accustomed to Tom's perverse ingenuity to laugh; he only smiled, and remarked with mock imdignation, — "Did she, though? the heartless huzzie!" Then he added, in a tone of melancholy expostulation, "Oh, Tom, Tom, do ye really think the Romans talked Bedlam? Do ye imagine that road-makers, and bridge-builders, and warriors, and law-givers such as they were, could talk sic blethers?"

Further disquisition was interrupted by a smart rap at the door, and John Dempster, who, in consideration of his grammatical ineffectiveness, was intrusted with the duty of opening the door, replenishing the ink-bottles, and a variety of other incidental employments, rose from his seat and lifted the "sneck." A handsome young fellow appeared in the doorway, clad in the blue uniform of a midshipman, and with his dirk by his side.

"Is that you, Watty — Mr Gordon, I mean?"—cried Andrew, delightedly. "Come in, come in. I'm blithe to see you."

The dazzling apparition of the young mid-shipman, as he complied with the invitation and stepped into the schoolroom, plunged the scholars into profound and admiring stupe-faction, till one boy, more adventurous than the rest, began to clap his hands softly, and Mr Prosser, far from repressing the sign of welcome, said with pedantic unction, "Vos plaudite"; and Walter, who had been a pupil in the school (he had once "shied" an ink-bottle at Mr Prosser's head — the mark was still upon the wall, "plain for all folk to see"), was greeted with uproarious applause. He returned the compliment by bowing gracefully, and with a heightened colour.

"Gang away to your seats, ye Latiners," said Mr Prosser, "and write out the verb *plaudo* in the first person plural of all the tenses, while I have a crack with my auld pupil."

The three accordingly retired, and Walter's eyes involuntarily followed the movements of the young girl with obvious interest and admiration.

"Are ye still on board the Hecla, Mr Gordon?" asked Mr Prosser.

"Yes, sir," was the smiling reply; "and we have had several brushes with the Johnny Crapauds."

Mr Prosser knitted his brows and shook his head.

"And of course you beat them," was his dry comment.

"Of course," said the youthful hero, proudly.

"They're a grand nation for all that," said Mr Prosser, in a low tone.

"What, sir!" exclaimed the young midshipman, "when they executed their king and queen—the bloodthirsty villains!"

" Well, but we executed Charles I.," re-marked Mr Prosser.

" Oh, that's a different case, you know," said Walter, confidently.

" Oh, of course ; we did it with an axe,—they did it with a guillotine. A very *sharp* distinction."

Walter laughed, and shook his head dubiously.

" How are your father and sister, Mr Gordon ? " Mr Prosser continued, pleasantly.

" Both very well, sir. My sister has be-come a monstrous fine lady, I assure you. I hardly knew her. You should hear her play on the guitar ; and how she does sing !—Italian and Spanish songs, *not* French, mind you."

" You haven't heard the ' Marseillaise,' I suppose ? "

" No, I have not. I prefer ' Rule Brit-annia,' " said Walter, with a frank smile.

" Yes, it's a braw song, especially when the ' ne-e-ever shall be slaves ' flutters and flaps like a jib when you are putting about."

Walter laughed gaily.

C

" That's good, sir.   I see you haven't forgot your seamanship."

" Oh, I am still a bit of a Palinurus."

" Who was he, sir, may I ask ? "

" Oh, Mr Gordon, have you forgot the
steersman of the Trojan fleet ? " asked Mr
Prosser, reproachfully.

" I have, sir.   I'm sure I beg his pardon.
But my Latin was always a purser's allowance, for which, of course, I have to thank
my own idleness."

" Well, how long are you to be ashore ? "

" I have a month's leave.   We are refitting at Portsmouth.   But I must not take
up your time, sir."   Then he added in a
whisper—

" You are still teaching Bella Simpson,
I see."

" Ay, she knows more about Palinurus
thán you do, Mr Gordon," was the whispered
reply.

" She always was a monstrous clever girl.
Is she still living with that smuggling uncle
of hers ? ".

" Yes ; and what's worse, that fuddling

randy of an aunt.   She's between Scylla and
Charybdis, puir lassie !   But she steers her
bark well ; she's well ballasted."

"Well, sir, good day to you.   I hope to
see you again soon," said Walter.

So saying, he shook hands heartily with
his former preceptor, and took his leave,
after a last fugitive glance at the young girl,
bent studiously over her desk.

CHAPTER II.

A MUSICAL EVENING AT THE MANSE.

WHEN afternoon school was over, Andrew Prosser took a short stroll, and then went up-stairs to his own apartments. These, as we have said, were three in number — a kitchen, bedroom, and little parlour. An elderly female, a widow, Mrs Badger by name, acted as his housekeeper nominally, but had gradually extended her functions till she had become his friend, mentor, doctor, spiritual adviser, and beneficent domestic tyrant. She was a tall, somewhat ungainly woman, with hard austere features. She was aggressively religious, and, as violent repudiation of Catholic infallibility generally implies a firm conviction of personal infallibility, she was extremely

dogmatic. She had originally belonged to
the Muggletonians, who believed that the
soul remains dormant till the resurrection ;
but after her husband's death she had
changed her creed and become a Baptist.
There being none of that sect in Fownie,
she went to the parish church, but always
stalked majestically out of her pew when
a baptism of infants took place, expressing
her dissent by contemptuous sniffs and a
grim and stony smile of derision. Andrew
often groaned under her domination, but
yielded to it on the whole submissively,
realising that probity and plausibility seldom
go together. And probity was the law of
Mrs Badger's being ; she husbanded his
resources more carefully than he would have
done himself, and higgled on his behalf with
an obstinacy and asperity which would have
spoiled the savour of his food had he known
of it. Between her and the fishwives in particular there raged a war " without herald
and without truce." Every haddock was
a skirmish, every cod a war-prize.

On reaching the top of the stairs, Andrew

tapped softly at the door, which was opened
after a decorous interval. " Wipe your feet
on the mat, Andrew," said Mrs Badger,
severely. " Your shoon are fair barkened
wi' glaur. Where have ye been ? "

" I took a bit turn along the road, and
the roads, like everything else in this down-
trodden country, are out o' order." And
Andrew shook his head with a look of
sour severity.

Mrs Badger gave a slight snort, and returned to the kitchen, whither she was followed by Andrew, after he had conscien-
tiously wiped his shoes. The kitchen was
spotlessly and finically clean. The deal-floor
bore only traces of " elbow-grease," as careful
housewives recommend ; the tins on the
dresser blinked gaily in the sunshine ; the
delf - ware beamed with homely cordiality ;
even the earthenware teapot, though black,
was comely. The light of the fire danced
on the polished fender, where the poker and
tongs reposed in state ; the duties of the one
implement being performed by a plebeian
iron rod leaning against one of the jambs,

and the other being so stiff with aristocratic idleness that, when it expanded, one limb remained fixed in paralytic rigidity, as if to assert its genteel helplessness; and Mrs Badger wisely supplied its services with her own hands, armed for the purpose with leathern gauntlets. A table covered with a coarse but snowy table-cloth stood in the middle of the apartment.

"What's for dinner to-day, Mrs Badger?" asked Andrew, anxiously.

"Sheep's-head broth," was the short and somewhat defiant reply.

"Ye ken I dinna like sheep's-head," murmured Andrew.

"Ye dinna like what's good for you," said Mrs Badger. "Its halesome, and sweet, and nourishing, and thrifty; and in these dear times——"

"Well, will ye give me a bit dram afterwards?" asked Andrew, compromising matters.

"If ye can find it in your heart to drink what I'm sure hasna paid its duty to the king——"

" *That* for the king!" said Andrew, with a derisive snap of the fingers. "The pampered loons get ower muckle of our goods and gear."

"Dinna speak evil o' dignities, Andrew," said Mrs Badger, severely.

"Dignities!" echoed Andrew, waving his horn-spoon with a rhetorical gesture. "Dignities are indignities;" and mollified by the felicity of his own remark, he proceeded to take his dinner without further parley.

His wholesome and thrifty meal being despatched, he began to cast covert and uneasy glances at a long clay pipe lying on the chimney-shelf.

"Take your pipe, Andrew," said Mrs Badger, with an air of grim toleration; " and when you're smoking, dinna forget to moraleese upon it. What says the godly poet?—

> ' All worldly stuff
> Gangs wi' a puff,
> Thus think and smoke tobacco;
> And when the bowl gets foul within,
> Think of your soul defiled wi' sin——' "

" Hoots, woman," interposed Andrew.

"One thing at a time. When I pray, I pray; when I smoke, I smoke; but piety and puffing is the queerest tobacco mixture I ever heard of. And, now, I'll hae my dram, if ye please."

"Smoke up the lum, then," said Mrs Badger, balancing the concession with a condition.

"Ay, ay, Mrs Badger, I see ye believe in a *quid pro quo*," remarked Andrew.

"If ye have any objection to make, speak out like a man," said Mrs Badger, bridling. "If that's Laetin, keep it where ye keep your stour—doon-stairs."

"Nae offence," said Andrew; "ye needna take a body up afore he falls."

When Andrew had finished his pipe, he took down a violin which was hanging on the wall, and tuned it. Then he struck up the revolutionary "Ça ira," the "Carmagnole," the "Marseillaise," and other melodies of the same kidney, which he played with much spirit and purity of tone, winding up with "God save the King," which he executed (that is probably the right word) with a good deal of raspiness and a variety of burlesque tremolos and cadenzas. Having thus given vent to his secret political sentiments, he stepped back into the kitchen with his instrument under his arm, and said, with a would-be jaunty air, which was a flagrant failure—

"I'm ganging to take a daunder down to the minister's, Mrs Badger; ye needna bide up for me."

"Very weel," rejoined Mrs Badger, with some asperity. "The minister and you are weel yokit thegither. He's a miserable Laodicean, and cares mair for reels and springs than the Psalms o' David."

"Hoots, awa," said Andrew; "David played on a harp, which is as much a stringed instrument as the fiddle. And, as for springs, ye ken he danced such a fandango that he scandalised a' the onlookers, and they werena *that* blate in those days."

"Dinna be profane, Andrew; ye ken he danced for holy joy, no for carnal gratification. The minister wad be better employed making a wheen new sermons; we're getting cauld kail het up again ower often to my thinking."

"A good tale is no the waur of being twice told, Mrs Badger."

"Use not vain repetitions as the heathen do," said Mrs Badger.

"You're aye heaving the Bible at folk's heads," said Andrew, a little impatiently. "Your texts are a' brickbats."

"Faithful are the wounds of a friend," retorted the irrepressible Mrs Badger.

"Aweel, I'll gang and get my wounds dressed," said Andrew, with a laugh.

"Beware of those, Andrew, that heal the wound slightly," rejoined Mrs Badger.

Andrew shrugged his shoulders, and quietly withdrew. For who can argue with a Concordance?

The manse stood at the end of the long and straggling street which passed through Fownie. It was enclosed by a stone wall of the statutory height, over which sycamores and horse-chestnuts hung their redundant foliage. A wooden door, painted green, gave access to the dwelling. A grassy sward, planted here and there with rhododendrons, stretched in front of the house ; and on the west side, and at the back, was a garden of hospitable size, in a corner of which was a little summer-house mantled with clematis. The garden was stocked with an abundance of old-fashioned flowers and medicinal herbs. Andrew sighed heavily as he pushed open the green door and entered. He tapped modestly at the front door ; and, after a short interval, it was opened by a young lady, who, on seeing Andrew, blushed faintly, and held out her hand with a gentle smile.

"Good evening, Miss Marjoribanks," said Andrew, softly.

"How do you do, Mr Prosser ? " she said, in a low melodious voice. "Papa is making a visit, but will be back presently. He thought you would come to-night," she went on with a smile ; "he said there was music in the air. Is there second hearing as well as second sight, I wonder ? Pray, come in.

Mamma has had a headache all day, and is resting for a little."

She seemed to be speaking so as to take the edge off a slight sense of embarrassment, which a woman out-manœuvres more skilfully than a man. She led the way to a little parlour, balmy with the scent of flowers. There was a harpsichord—probably the only one in Fownie,—and a violoncello leaned in a tipsy attitude—'tis the Silenus of musical instruments—against a corner.

Andrew untied the silk-handkerchief wrapped round his violin, and laid the instrument on the table. Then he sat down in an arm-chair, with a preoccupied and pensive look on his honest and manly features.

"It is nearly a fortnight since you were here last," said Miss Marjoribanks, in a playfully reproachful tone. "You know you need never wait for an invitation. Your violin is your passport," she added, as if by way of afterthought.

"I have not been in good spirits," said Andrew, looking at her with a troubled look in his large dark eyes.

" Then you should have tried King Saul's remedy.   Nothing serious, I hope ? "

" Nothing exceptionally so.   A *poor* man's troubles are chronic."

A little colour came and went in her pale cheeks.   With a woman's delicate intuition she divined the motive for his remark.

" I think everybody is poor nowadays," she said, gently.   " These dreadful wars——— "

" Say rather the tyranny of kings and the wasteful luxury of nobles and land-owners who batten on the toil of the people," said Andrew, in a harsh vibrating voice; for on this subject he was always fierce and acrimonious.   Speculative anti-pathies indeed are more intense and im-placable than personal ones, and perhaps no one is so truculent as a humanitarian.

" Homer calls the king the shepherd of the people," continued Andrew; " nowadays he would call him the butcher of the people. What are we?   Sheep for the slaughter, after we have first been well shorn.   But it will not last, Miss Marjoribanks.   The Seine will flow into the Thames."

"I hope not, Mr Prosser," said Miss Marjoribanks, earnestly. "Its waters are red with blood and salt with human tears."

"Tyranny, when it grows to a plethora, needs blood - letting," said Andrew, vehemently. "I grant you the French Revolution has been a violent remedy. A people brutalised by oppression acts brutally. The rulers of France sowed the wind, and have reaped the whirlwind. But, as Andrew Marvell says of our own Revolution in the time of Charles I., the French Revolution

'To all lands not free
Shall climacteric be.'"

"I have no wish to discuss such subjects," said Miss Marjoribanks, somewhat coldly. "But I would earnestly warn you, Mr Prosser, to beware of what you say to those you are not absolutely sure of. But here comes papa," and she rose from her seat with an obvious air of relief.

Mr Marjoribanks entered the room. He was tall and somewhat gaunt, his cheeks a little sunken, and his shoulders rounded, but the brightness of his deep - blue eyes

and the fresh colour of his mobile lips in-
dicated an abundant store of vitality. The
fine contour and ample size of his forehead
were rendered more conspicuous by his bald-
ness.

"A sicht o' you, Andrew, is guid for sair
een," he said, with a winning smile, as he
came forward and shook Mr Prosser heartily
by the hand. "So you have brought your
fiddle," and taking up the instrument he
thrummed the strings in a pizzicato style
as he went on talking.

"I have just seen Bella Simpson, Milly;
she is turning a beautiful girl. I wish we
could get her away from her uncle's. Not
that Simpson is a bad fellow; he is a very
regular hearer, and a bit of a theologian;
but that inn of his harbours queer customers.
Then his wife—it's sad, very sad."

"I think Bell might with proper training
become a good teacher of music," said Miss
Marjoribanks. "She has an enchanting
voice."

"She sings as if she were 'quiring to the
young-eyed cherubim,'" said Mr Marjori-

banks. "Oh, why is it, Andrew, that truth has not such a soul-subduing organ? Don't you think she would make anybody good if she merely *sang* the Ten Commandments, while I — never mind. Crows are needed as well as nightingales, I suppose."

"She has got a famous headpiece," said Andrew, with professional enthusiasm. "She's as far as cube root in arithmetic, and quadratics in algebra, and she's uncommonly clear about the use of the subjunctive mood, which is, as you know, Mr Marjoribanks, a crucial test of Latinity."

"It is, as I know to my cost," said Mr Marjoribanks, the right corner of his mouth descending in a humorous smile. "But never mind Latin; it's dead, and it's a pity that it isn't decently buried, with a *Requiescat in pace* engraved upon its tombstone, expressing the pious aspirations of schoolboys. Tune up your fiddle, while I go and freshen myself with a wash."

Miss Marjoribanks sat down to the harpsichord, and gave Andrew his A, embroidering it with softly sounded chords, till his instru-

ment was in tune; and then she glided into
the sweet old melody, " There grows a
bonnie briar - bush in oor kailyard," while
Andrew supplied a dexterous " vamp," as
he called it.

The minister now reappeared, and got his
'cello in order.

" We'll give a sop to Cerberus, Andrew,
and play a few sacred pieces at first, while
folks are stirring about.   People call me the
' fiddling minister,' which is much worse than
being a ' fuddling minister,' mind you; so
we'll strike up some of the songs of Zion
—eh, Andrew ?   What say you to ' Now
Israel may say ' ? "

" It's a grand tune," said Andrew—" a
kind of Covenanting march."

" Then we might try ' Adeste Fideles.'
Why do you smile, Milly ?   I didn't invent
the title.   After that—it's well to have a
programme — we might take the glorious
minuet from Handel's ' Saul,' then—sound
your A again, Andrew."

The programme was duly carried out and
liberally extended, with intervals of soci-

able conversation; and by ten o'clock, after various delicate and cautious gradations of selection, the musical rehearsal tapered off with reels and strathspeys. At about eleven o'clock Andrew left the manse. The village was buried in profound stillness, and he could hear with absolute distinctness the waves plashing on the shore, and the rattle and clash of the pebbles sucked back by the undertow. It was a very dark night, and as Andrew turned into the lane leading to the schoolhouse, he came suddenly into collision with the burly figure of a man. Andrew, with instant exasperation—for his nerves were still tingling with musical excitement—gave the man a vindictive push, for which he was rewarded with a growling imprecation.

"Oh, is it you, Simpson?" said Andrew, recognising Simpson's favourite expletive.

"Mr Prosser!" exclaimed the other, with an abrupt transition to marked civility of tone. "My excuses. It's fell dark the nicht; I'm wae for the revenue cutters— baith them and the free - traders will be

droppin' *anchors* this nicht ; " and he gave
a significant laugh. " Weel, weel, we maun
a' live."

" I have something to say to you, Simpson," said Andrew, lowering his voice. " Come
on to the bents with me."

CHAPTER III.

A TALK ON THE BENTS.

THE two men went along the bents, approaching at the same time the shore. A dilapidated upturned boat lay on the margin of the grassy slope, and sitting down, they leaned their backs against it. For a minute or two they listened to the rhythmic plash of the waves, and the random gusts of wind filling the waste places of the night. Andrew had fallen into a reverie, probably a melancholy one, for he sighed when he was roused by Simpson's question—

"Well, what is it, Andrew?"

Andrew cleared his throat.

"Ye ken, Simpson, that I have been whiles

useful to you and your clanjamfry o' dare-devils."

"I ken that, Mr Prosser," said the other, with gruff heartiness. "And ye .can aye get a keg o' spirits when ye give me the hint."

"Oh, I'm aware ye are always willing to *liquidate* your obligations," said Andrew. "But drinking is not much in my line—beyond a post-prandial dram, that is; and if I wink at your on-goings, and even at times lend ye a helping hand, ye may be sure I have other reasons. I'll maybe tell ye what they are when I can lippen to ye."

"Eh, Mr Prosser, but that's hard," said Simpson in an aggrieved tone.

"Smuggling, Simpson, is no exactly a school for a' the virtues, ye see, and I must be cautious. In these sair times everybody is living in a whispering gallery, with the Secretary o' State at the one focus, and the President of the Court o' Session at the other. However, that's Greek to you, Simpson. What I mean is, that it's safest to take soundings when ye're in an unknown bay.

You may be shallow or you may be deep,—
but my metaphors are getting fankled.
Well, now, I saw Gillespie, the preventive
officer, last night."

Simpson muttered an angry oath.

"Do you think he jalooses anything about
our next venture?" he asked, anxiously.

"Bide a wee, and I'll tell you a' about it.
You must know I was taking a daunder
along the shore about ten o'clock. It was
gey and dark,—I think, Simpson, you must
have the power the Thessalian witches had
of drawing down the moon,—well, I had just
got as far as the Deil's Mash-tub, and was
standing looking doon into it — the tide
was full, and the waves were churning and
boiling in it—when I found myself gruppit
from behind by the collar of my coat. I
thought at first that somebody—maybe auld
Clootie himsel' — wanted to push me into
the infernal caldron, and my very hair
stiffened wi' the gliff I got. Fortunately
for mysel', I'm not an easy customer to
tackle——"

Simpson gave a croaking laugh.

"That's true, Mr Prosser. I'm thinking you could gar the Pert Polly's anchor come hame, if you took a haul at the cable."

"Porritch and sobriety does it," said Andrew, complacently. "If ye lift your little finger ower often, you'll lift nothing else afore long. And tea is nearly as bad. Our women never had the vapours till tea came in fashion."

"I never could thole sic watery blash," said Simpson, with much emphasis.

"I ken ye prefer *strong* waters," remarked Andrew. "But if, as Dr Johnson says, 'Who drives fat oxen should himself be fat,' it does not follow logically that he who drinks strong waters should himself be strong. However, this is a digression. When I found myself gruppit, I let out a backward kick, that garred the fellow yell like a demoniac. He let go his hold, and I turned round and faced him. It was Gillespie, and he was standing on one leg like a drookit hen, and holding the other with both hands, and swearing—well, if the deil himsel' had come out of his Mash-tub,

he couldna have improved upon it. 'What
do you mean,' said I, 'collaring a man like
that? Can a man no take a walk by the
shore — which, mind you, belongs to the
people and no to the blood-sucking land-
owners — without being mishandled by an
officer of excise?' 'I know you, Andrew
Prosser,' says he, gnashing his teeth; 'you're
hand in glove wi' the smugglers. You're
here to make private signals.' I gave a
laugh at that. 'I'm here as a lover of
Nature,' said I, 'and I'm wae to see that
her fairest scenes are defaced by officers of
excise. Gang hame, John; ye have found
a mare's nest this time, and tasted the
quality of her hoofs forby.' 'I'll chalk
that kick up ahint the door, Prosser,' says
he, 'and you'll pay for it. I hae my eye
upon you.' 'A cat may look at a king,
nae doot,' said I; 'sae lang as ye keep
your hands aff me, you may glower your
een oot o' your heid.' 'Bide a wee, my
braw billy,' says he; 'I'll make a clean
sweep of you all afore lang. You're ower
intimate wi' Simpson to be an honest man'

—ye see, Simpson, ye're mair famed for the smell o' brandy than the odour of sanctity——"

"The deil thraw the neck o' him!" muttered Simpson, indignantly.

"Amen! but ye'll have to be cautious, for I think he has got secret information. Somebody's tap is running."

This intimation appeared to alarm Simpson considerably. "Who can it be?" he muttered. "If I knew——" And he supplied the hiatus by clenching his formidable fist, and growling some very vigorous imprecations.

"So much for that matter," said Andrew, "and if I see any danger looming I'll let you know. And now, I have another subject to discuss with you."

"It's getting late," said Simpson, in slightly muffled tones, "and the raw air is bad for my rheumatics."

"Yours is an accommodating rheumatism, Simpson," said Andrew. "However, I winna insist. Only, mind ye, the subject has got to be faced sune or syne."

"Oh, very well, then; a wilfu' man will hae his way. What is it?"

"Nobody can say, Simpson, that I am a busybody. I have too much respect for the liberty of the—citizen. A man's habits are his own, even if they're bad. A hallan-shaker has a right to his rags, as a merchant to his broadcloth; and sumptuary laws, moral as well as physical, I'm dead against. But if a man's ways threaten to injure those I am bound to protect, then I step in. A sweep has a right to his sooty clothes; but I wadna let him gang among my tidy bit lassies and smudge their clean pinafores. I'm *in loco parentis* to my pupils; and if a parent, relative, or guardian neglects his or her duties, then I interfere. A neglected child is virtually an orphan, and an orphan should find a father in every good man, and a mother in every kind - hearted woman. Now, to apply these principles, which are maybe rather above your comprehension, for your liquid capacity is greater than your mental, I doubt——"

"Maybe I'm no as dull as ye think," said

Simpson, a little sullenly. "I canna talk like you. You could talk the hind-leg aff a horse—a horse?—an elephant! But I hae my thochts, deep anes——"

"Ower deep, I'm thinking," said Andrew.

"But my words aye gang to leeward o' my ideas."

"Well, well, you may be a 'mute in- glorious Milton' for me, Simpson; but I'm gangin' to leeward of *my* subject. You have a niece who is my pupil."

"I hae, and a braw lass she is, though I say it that shouldna."

"Why should you not?"

"Weel, ye see, being a relative——"

"Yes, that's just it. What relative is she? Is she your niece or your wife's?"

"She's my brother's daughter," said Simp- son, after a short pause.

"She is not what is ironically called a love- child, eh? You'll excuse the question."

"No, no; *that's* a' richt!" said Simpson, emphatically. "She was born in holy wed- lock."

"Good. Is her father dead?"

"Dead as Methusalem. He was a captain in the merchant service, and was drowned when his ship was wrecked on one of the Scilly Islands. Puir Archie! He was a braw lad—muckle handsomer than me."

"That's highly probable; and his wife must have been a bonnie woman, judging by Bell,—for I must confess I can only see her likeness to you 'tanquam in speculo,' in a glass, *very* darkly."

"Ay, ay, Bessie was a braw lass," said Simpson, with a laboured sigh. "But all flesh is grass. And noo, I think I'll e'en take the road hame."

"Man alive!" cried Andrew, with unbounded surprise, "I have only just begun. All this has only been a kind of preface or preamble."

"Well, well," said Simpson, gruffly. "Sae be it. Only haul closer to windward, gin ye please."

"Tom Simpson," said Andrew, solemnly, "it's no easy matter to get the weather-gage of you."

Simpson gave a hoarse chuckle.

" Maybe no," he said.

" Well, I'll come a few points nearer the wind," continued Andrew, significantly. " My question is this : What do ye mean to do with Bell ? "

" To give her a guid education first,—and I believe that there's no a schoolmaster in the country can carry her on as weel as you can, Mr Prosser."

" Who is steering wild now ? " asked Andrew, ignoring the ingratiating remark. " A good education is a means to an end. What's the end in her case ? "

" Weel, she'll be handy in the hoose. My wife is unco fond o' her."

" We are getting on to delicate ground now," said Andrew. " But I'll ask you a question : Is your wife fit to look after a young lassie growing up into womanhood ? Dinna answer me unless ye like : it's no business of mine directly. But I have heard of blows given——"

" She's no hersel' when the fit is on her," said Simpson, in a low tone. " She's fair red wud. A bear robbed o' its whelps is a small comparison. But eh! she's sorry after-hin. She has a big heart as well as a big body. And then she's English, ye ken. We shouldna judge her by oor standard."

"Well, passing that, do ye mean to say that ye mean to keep her in that boosing-kain of yours? Ye ken the sort of talk that's to be heard there, and the wild on-goings of your harum-scarum companions."

"Their bark is waur than their bite. I would rather lippen her to them than to fine city bucks and macaronis. Besides, I'm there to protect her——"

"'Quis custodiet ipsos custodes?'" muttered Andrew, grimly.

"Na, na, Mr Prosser; she's safe enough wi' me. I ken a wheen lassies that would hae been better serving stoups o' ale than waiting at table. Brose and broth disna coup the stamack, and that's what the diet they get at some grand hooses does for the puir misguidit limmers."

"There's some truth in that, Simpson," said Andrew. "But observe: life in an ale-house would be misery to Bell. She isn't

made of the same clay as you or me.   Now,
you have taken charge of her, and you are
responsible for her peace of mind, her happiness, and her prospects.   Who would marry
her out of an alehouse?   I mean, what man
worthy of her beauty, her talents, and her
virtues?   No, no; you must put her somewhere else than among your pint-stoups.
Ye dinna plant a rose-tree in a midden,
do ye?"

"That's a braw comparison, by my certy!"
exclaimed Simpson, indignantly.

"Comparisons *are* sometimes odorous," remarked Andrew, composedly.   "Reason it
out, Simpson; you have got to find a proper
sphere for her."

"Orphans hae nae call to be pernickety,"
said Simpson, a little sullenly.   "And it
wad be wrong to gie her ideas abune her
station."

"Station!" cried Andrew, hotly.   "Nature knows nothing about station.   Rank,
titles, coronets, and crowns are man's silly
work.   But Nature means that her ladies
and gentlemen (who are oftener clad in

homespun than in purple and fine linen)
should live according to their station as
fixed by *her:* to wit, that good brains
should have a chance of free activity, and
virtue not be stained by the propinquity of
vice. If we treated men and women as we
treat our cabbages and potatoes and roses
and lilies, humanity would be a garden of
the Lord. And that good time is coming.
We are making a beginning on the other
side of the Channel. A Tree of Freedom
has been planted, whose leaves are for the
healing of the nations. But this is a digression. You'll mind, Simpson, that Bell
is one of Nature's ladies, and you have got
to respect that fact. Forby that, she is
well educated. She can read Virgil and
Horace. You would set her to clean pint-
stoups, would you? I tell ye, Simpson, it's
high treason against Nature! And that's
the only treason that I reprobate."

"Ye seem unco fond o' her," remarked
Simpson, with a gruff laugh.

"I love her as her father might have
done," said Andrew, solemnly. "I have

taught her since she was a wee bit toddlin'
bairn. I mind the very twist o' her bonny
mou' when she said *a-b, ab.* There's nothing
but goodness and truth and sweetness in
her heart. Foul fa' the man that wrongs
her!"

"To my thinking," said Simpson, as if
struck by a luminous idea, "you should wait
for twa or three years and marry her yoursel'.
I'm sure, we would be prood o' the match,
and it would be the only way o' convincing
you that she's only a woman. It's wunnerfu'
how angels *afore* marriage take the moult
after marriage."

"Ye have paid me a compliment, Simpson, in proposing sic a thing," said Andrew,
gravely. "But observe! though I care
nothing for human rank, and for that
matter would think myself good enough
for a duchess,—that's not pride, for I regard a duchess only as a woman, and I'll
be bound a duchess wants a man first, and
a duke next,—but I respect *natural* distinctions; for all men are not equal in the sight
of Nature, more's the pity, and what we

should aim at,—dinna fidge aboot, this is better than counting a tavern score,—what we should aim at is to make Nature's Cinderellas Nature's princesses, raise the standard of the race till all are equal in a natural sense—equal, I say, not uniform, just as I saw this spring some beds of primroses in the minister's garden all equal in a sense, but all distinct in pattern and colouring, some patterns and colours rarer than others, and so more frail and delicate, as not yet hardened to a type,—for example, lilac primroses. Have you ever seen a lilac primrose, Simpson? I needna ask you; but it's a finer sight than the Pert Polly sneaking into the Giant's Elbow with a hundred kegs of Hollands in her hold. But I *am* gangin' to leeward this time. What I mean is, Bell is far above me——"

Simpson's attention, which had been manifestly wandering, became at once concentrated.

"You're ower blate," he interposed, hastily.

" No; I am just, that's all. She is a princess in disguise. I could never educate myself up to her level."

" Havers ! " said Simpson.

" Truth ! Where did she get her refinement, her unconscious grace like a fawn's ? her innocent but noble gaze ? her simple courtesy ? never bold, but never abashed ; modest but never awkward ; never haughty, but yet the very turn of her neck is stately, and, as the Latin poet says, ' incedit regina,' she walks like a queen."

" By my certy ! " exclaimed Simpson, with a burst of laughter too boisterous to be quite spontaneous. " Like Paul, much learning hath made thee mad."

" I am not mad, most noble Simpson," rejoined Andrew, with a short dry laugh. " Come, now, who was her mother ? A lady ? for birth as yet unfortunately means breeding."

" She came of a good stock, I believe," said Simpson. " But I must leave you. Ye hae preached me a lang sermon, and my brains are fair bizzin'."

" Very well; but mind, my sermon has got an application. Think it over, and let me ken what you ettle to do with her. I'll help you, if I can."

" I will, Mr Prosser, I will," said Simpson with alacrity. " Guid nicht. It's lang past elders' hours."

" Good nicht," replied Andrew, mechanically.

He stood for some time wrapt in meditation, and then muttered to himself, " There's some secret aboot the lassie's birth. He has been like a hen on a hot girdle for the last half-hour."

He sat down on the boat, and probably his thoughts had fixed themselves on Miss Marjoribanks, for he sighed heavily now and then. At last he rose and wended his way slowly homewards. As he softly opened the door, Mrs Badger's voice from the closet where she slept smote his ears, and made him start nervously.

" Ye keep braw hours, Andrew. Where hae ye been ? "

"I have been studying a problem, Mrs Badger," was the reply. "I've been trying to find x."

"The clock has lang syne chappit twal," was the injured remark.

"Let it chap," said Andrew, impatiently; "that's what it's for."

CHAPTER IV.

THE HOLY WELL.

BEECHGROVE HALL, the residence of Mr
Gordon, Walter's father, stood a mile in-
land from the village. It was an old
house, lofty for its width, with high-
pitched roofs and turret-like projections at
the angles of the walls. It was reached
from the road by a fine avenue of beeches;
and standing near the middle of a long
acclivity, it commanded an extensive view
of the surrounding country.

Mr Gordon had been a navy contractor,
and had amassed a large fortune while he
was still comparatively in the prime of life.
His wife had died shortly after the birth
of his only daughter Sibylla, who was two

years younger than Walter. Though only sixteen years of age, she seemed already a young woman—this precocious physical development being probably due to the fact that her mother had been a Creole.

It was the breakfast hour of the day after Walter's arrival, and his father and he were standing at the window chatting together till Sibylla should make her appearance. Mr Gordon was a stout handsome man, whose whole appearance, his massive and yet well-proportioned frame, his grave and deliberate movements, the level steadiness of his voice, and the dignity of his look, conveyed an impression of moral stability and repose, which contrasted strikingly with the gay vivacity of his son. And yet the youth had his father's powerful brow, and his expressive and mobile features when at rest settled into the same placid gravity. His face had a healthy paleness, with a faint olive tinge, suggestive of the Creole blood in his veins; but he had his father's dark blue eyes, with specks of hazel round the iris.

"Good morning, gentlemen," said a playful voice; and as father and son turned
round, Sibylla—for it was she—made an
elaborate curtsey, full of sportive grace.

Her father imprisoned her soft cheeks
within his large shapely white hands and
kissed her on the brow; and Walter, imi-
tating her roguish humour, took her hand
and raised it to his lips with an air of
courtly homage.

"Ten minutes late, Miss Indolence," said
Mr Gordon, smilingly consulting his watch
as he took his seat at the table.

"'Tis deep design, papa; your hunger
makes me sure of a welcome. Good morning, John."

This salutation was addressed to Mr
Gordon's man-servant, John Wilkie, who
waited at table. He was a tall elderly
man, with a rugged weather-beaten face;
his lower eyelids were seamed with a net-
work of fine wrinkles, and his eyes wore
that peering and yet far-away look—the
reflection of the mystery of the sea—which
sailors acquire who have for long years

been in the habit of scanning distant horizons and misty stretches of ocean. He had a wooden leg, and wore a long pig-tail tied with a bow of black ribbon.

He had been boatswain on board the frigate Resistance under Captain King, and had lost his right leg below the knee in the spirited action fought between that vessel and the French frigate La Coquette in the year 1783 near Turk's Island. He had been pensioned, and had returned to his native village of Fownie, where Mr Gordon had made his acquaintance and taken him into his service. He had proved an invaluable servant, obedient without servility as a true man-of-war's-man, and punctiliously honest as befits a man with a wooden leg, who, from the emphasis and noisy assertion of his walk, has lost the capacity for furtive and sneaking movements. He idolised his young mistress, and while mechanically respectful to his master, was on quarter-deck behaviour with the young midshipman, doffing his cap to him in season and out of

season. Poor John! he knew nothing of
natural equality and the rights of man;
and if any one had tried to indoctrinate
him with these fine French notions, he
would probably have squirted his tobacco-
juice with vicious energy and growled his
contempt for the Johnny Crapauds and
their frivolous and fantastic notions.

John returned the morning salutation of
his mistress in a voice like the rumble of a
carronade, though his eyes brightened and his
features assumed a grim and dislocated smile.

Sibylla was a charming and engaging
sight, as she sat at the head of the table
behind the tea-urn, dressed in a dainty white
muslin gown, her taper fingers hovering over
the cups as she dispensed the hospitalities
of the breakfast-table. Her cheeks had the
same olive tinge as her brother's, her hair
and eyebrows were dark; but her eyes, like
her brother's, were blue—a piquant contrast,
which lent a strange and bewildering charm
to her features. The arch smiling face had
the soft loveliness, the almost porcelain delicacy, of a portrait by Greuze; but if any

critic of physiognomy had observed that face
while her father said grace, he would have
been struck by the complete change of expression, due to the absolute correspondence
between feeling and its outward manifesta-
tion, which resulted in what might be called
physical honesty. The Hebe had become a
nun, the maiden *à la* Greuze was transformed
into a Madonna *à la* Murillo. Her face, indeed, with the eyes closed and the lips gently
pressed together, might have served as a
model for that of some virgin confessor, the
more so that in repose it bore the imprint of
a haunting and unconscious pathos, a dim
foreshadowing of sorrow.

After the conversation had touched on a
number of indifferent topics, Walter said
suddenly—

" Speaking of the people I met yesterday,
there was one whom I don't happen to
know."

" What sort of a person ? " asked Mr
Gordon.

" A gentleman, rather dark-complexioned,
the cheeks and chin close-shaven, and with

a long black moustache. He was riding on a handsome chestnut in the direction of Swinton. You know I had gone to see my old nurse, and I met him on the way back. He looked inquisitively at me for a moment or two, and then honoured me with an almost imperceptible salutation."

"Who could it be, John?" asked Mr Gordon, with some show of interest.

"Lord Wimpole, sir," said John, in a matter-of-fact tone.

"Ah, to be sure," rejoined Mr Gordon; "Lord Wimpole of Swinton Hall, Walter. I heard that he had recently arrived, and meant to stay for a few months. I must give him a call."

"Is it socially possible for you to visit a live lord, papa?" asked Sibylla, half jocularly. "Is it not the case that etiquette, like the tide, only goes up a certain distance, and that the nobility are above high-water mark? I would not like you to be snubbed."

"Lord Wimpole is as little likely to snub me as I am to take a snubbing, my dear," said Mr Gordon.

"Well, he looks as if he was quite capable of being arrogant," remarked Walter. "He is just like the captain of an Algerine felucca or a Spanish xebeque : these fellows often have the same air of dusky picturesque dare-devilry. But what is he? who is he? what is he doing here?"

"I don't know much about him," replied his father. "I understand he has obtained his estate and title from some collateral branch. In his younger days I believe he was in one of the services—army or navy, I don't know which. He has the reputation of having led a somewhat unsettled life."

"Is he married, sir?" asked Walter.

"I believe not. But it is hardly in good taste to talk about him in this way. Did you see Mr Prosser, Walter?"

"Oh yes," replied Walter, with a smile. "He is just as delightfully whimsical as ever."

"There are strange rumours about him, Watty," remarked Sibylla, earnestly.

"My dear Sibylla!" exclaimed Walter, incredulously.

"It is quite true, dear, though possibly it is mere detraction. People insinuate that he is not a loyal subject, that he harbours seditious projects, and is even a member of a secret society imbued with revolutionary principles. He is also said to be in league with smugglers; but, to be sure, that is nothing, for in that matter few have clean hands. Even I do not too curiously trace the peregrinations of the lace that reaches me."

"But what grounds have they for accusing him of disloyalty?" asked Walter, anxiously.

"Nay, I know not; but he talks strangely at times, and he plays the 'Ça ira,' and suchlike songs, on his fiddle."

"There's no sedition in a fiddle," said Walter. "You are not a papist because you play 'Ave Marias' on your harpsichord."

"I have dutifully taken my religion from papa, who knows best, and whose goodness commends his religion; but, if I may be frank, I have my leanings towards the Catholic Church. Our dear mamma was a Catholic;" and her eyes filled with tears.

" May you always be as good as she was, my dear," said Mr Gordon, a little huskily. " But we won't speak about such matters, which pertain to the individual conscience. We must not identify religion either with superstition or bigotry, which are its eastward and westward shadows. I, too, have heard of Mr Prosser's proceedings, and you should advise him to be careful, Walter. I am a justice of the peace, and I might have an unpleasant duty to perform. Now I shall leave you. I have some letters to write."

" What do you say to a walk, Sibylla ? " asked Walter.

" 'Tis not often I have the prospect of so gallant an escort," said Sibylla, gaily. " I shall be delighted."

And she left the room to dress.

" Is there anything in this, sir ? " asked Walter, as his father rose from the table.

" I fear it greatly ; and in times like these even lukewarmness is veiled treason. Warn your friend. I should not like him to come to harm."

In an incredibly short time for a young

lady, Sibylla reappeared equipped for her walk. She was dressed in a gown of French cambric, and a Flemish mantle of twilled sarsenet,—so might loveliness be attired in those distant days, — while a chip hat, trimmed with jonquille ribbon, adorned her head.

"By Neptune and his trident!" exclaimed Walter, gaily, as he surveyed his sister, "you are monstrous fine. What fashion-plate have you walked out of?"

"Nay, keep your compliments for some other young lady, and don't beggar yourself in flatteries, or, as flattery is woman's ambrosia, some young damsel will have to starve for want of it."

Walter's cheeks reddened a little, and he gave an embarrassed laugh.

"Where would you like to go?" he asked.

"There is an old well in the skirts of Swinton Wood which I sometimes visit. It was, and is still indeed, regarded as a holy well, of much medicinal virtue; but Mr Marjoribanks says it is ferruginous, and that the Virgin has nothing to do with it—though,

perhaps, mind you, iron needs a blessing as
much as ordinary food. Be that as it may,
'tis a pretty spot, though grievously neglected. And yet its very dilapidation has a
pathetic charm. It is a symbol of decayed
faith. How many people long generations
ago visited the well with pious hopes! And
they have long since departed, but still the
water flows. How vain is our life, how
evanescent our joys and sorrows!"

"Very true, no doubt; but we have got
to live our life, as these people lived theirs.
And in my profession it is a fine thing that
death is as much honoured as life, so that
we get the full good of our existence."

"You have been in several actions, dearest,"
said Sibylla, tenderly. "How many is it?"

"Counting the big ones and the little
whets and *divertissements*, I have been in
seven," said Walter, a little self-complacently.

"Were you not afraid?"

"I was too much afraid of being afraid to
think much of the danger. Ah, but if you
saw our captain! What a hero he is! He
goes into action as if he were going to a ball."

With such talk they beguiled the way till they reached the well. A little footpath diverging from the road led to a circular space embowered in elms and mountain-ashes. The wooded slope here abruptly terminated in a rugged face of rock, from a fissure in the middle of which issued a runnel of water, that flowed down into a stone trough stained a reddish yellow, and felted on the outside with the greenest moss. A decayed plank lay over the tiny channel by which the water escaped to some neighbouring brook. Nothing could be more inviting than the soothing murmur and gurgle of the tiny stream ; and brother and sister seated themselves on a tree-trunk which had been uprooted by a storm, and lay athwart the rounded hollow.

There was a dreamy spell about the scene which predisposed to silence, and Sibylla's face had assumed a look of pensive melancholy, when her musings were interrupted by a question addressed to her—

"Sibylla, dear, what mean those little bits of crimson worsted or cloth tied round the branches of the rowan - tree opposite us ? "

" Every strip means a maiden's heart long-ing to be occupied," replied Sibylla, with a smile. " It is an old, old superstition. Girls who want a husband (and they are perchance more numerous than those who don't) fasten up these as reminders to the gentle patron of the well ; at least, that is the origin of the superstitious rite. And so they speak ' good painted cloth,' though they confide the secret only to this same patron. The strip must be the colour of their heart's blood, and the berries of the tree may fancifully symbolise drops of blood. So I interpret. Indeed we are wrong if we think there was little imagin-ation in these old times. To my thinking, it is we who are unimaginative."

" Well, Sibylla, you need offer no such vows ; your face makes you sure of many suitors."

" Only my face ? " repeated Sibylla, with a blush and in a reproachful tone.

" Yes, your face—that is, your eloquent face ; but I must not forestall your suitors."

"Believe me, Watty, my wishes are not commonplace in such a matter. Even to a brother I may not speak of such things, but I foresee that if I purchase happiness, it will be at a heavy cost; and indeed, I think I have been born to prove in my experience the most essential sweetness of sorrow."

"You have your meaning, doubtless; but I don't grasp it," said Walter, with a laugh. "You are too subtle for a plain sailor like me."

"Emotions have their metaphysics. Heigho! this comes of reading Milton and Shakespeare. For one thing, Watty, I shall never marry a fool. Let him be wicked, wild, tempestuous, or blasted with misfortune and at odds with fortune and his fellow-men—there is my sphere; but heaven defend me from a fool, however good he be, if it be possible to be a fool and yet good, which I greatly doubt."

"A romantic notion, dear Sibylla. You must not throw yourself away on any one less worthy than yourself."

"A fig for such prudent notions," said Sibylla, impetuously. "Is it not far nobler for a woman to raise and redeem a man? I do not admire the woman who has every virtue except that of self-sacrifice. And she is but a Pharisee who prizes her own perfection so highly that she will not look at a man less virtuous than herself. What is virtue worth if it has not courage? When you, good brother, encounter a sinking ship, you do not think of the characters of the perishing mariners. Even if they were pirates, I believe you would try to rescue them."

"Yes; and we would probably hang them afterwards."

"That is as may be. But, in the first place, you would give them a glimpse of the humanity they had disowned, and so prepare them for repentance. We profess to be Christians; but surely the first duty of a Christian is to seek and save those that are lost."

"Would you marry a bad man, Sibylla?"

"What do you mean by a bad man? Does a really bad man exist?"

" I have met a good few in my short experience of life," replied Walter, with a laugh.

" Pooh, my dear, what do you know of the men whom you knock on the head ? Perhaps, indeed, a woman should not marry a man who is manifestly depraved, who has become one of Circe's hogs ; but if she meets and loves a man who, amidst all his errors, has still some glimmer of the heavenly light, she should be bold and adventurous enough, I think, to share her goodness with him. His love will be all the greater for his gratitude. A wife who is also a Madonna has a double chance of adoration. But perhaps this is not the sort of talk that befits a good and virtuous female ! "

" I must always strike my flag when I have an argument with you, Sibylla. That comes of staying at home and reading Milton and Shakespeare, as you said. And that suggests to me that I saw Imogen lately."

" Ah, Walter, I know whom you mean. Is your heart still anchored there ? "

"Oh, I am not a sighing swain," said Walter, blushing. "And yet she is — she is——"

"Infinitely engaging is, I believe, the modish phrase," said Sibylla, laughing.

"She seems vastly improved—I mean in refinement and so on."

"The reason is not far to seek," said Sibylla, gaily, "for she associates with me."

"How kind of you, Sibylla!"

"Oh, do not suppose that I am acting as lapidary on your account. Bell and I are bosom-friends, because we love one another. Nor do I think it any derogation on my part, for nobody believes that Simpson is her uncle."

"Perhaps it would be better if he were," said Walter, gloomily.

"Her birth is no doubt a mystery; but, I am prone to think, no ignoble one. Or else, whence her instinctive goodness? And she has dim memories of a lovely and tender mother. Simpson and his wife are farming her, I do suspect."

"This should be looked to."

"And so it shall, if I live," said Sibylla, energetically.

"She is very clever, is she not?"

"She is musical to the tips of her fingers. Do you know she will sit down to the harpsichord and play any song she hears, though she does not know a single note?"

"Why don't you teach her?"

"She prefers to hear me play," said Sibylla, with a slight shade of embarrassment. "Besides, she is very modest, and does not wish to acquire accomplishments which she avers are beyond her station. Perhaps she is right, after all; for indeed, even common girls have sometimes uncommon beauty."

At this point their conversation was interrupted by the sound of approaching footsteps, and, turning their heads, they saw a tall gentleman come striding up the path.

He was handsomely dressed, and had an air of inbred distinction. Seeing the two young people, he courteously raised his hat and said, "I crave your pardon," in somewhat untuneful but cultivated accents.

Walter rose to his feet and stiffly returned the salutation.

"There are no intruders, sir, where all are free to come," he said coldly, for he had recognised Lord Wimpole.

"I bethink me," said that gentleman, "that I have the honour of addressing Miss Gordon and her brother."

Sibylla rose and curtseyed politely. She cast a woman's comprehensive glance upon him, and confessed to herself that, though he was not a handsome man, he possessed attractions superior to merely physical beauty. He must have been at least thirty - five years of age, and his form had reached its acme of strength and vigour. His features were somewhat rudely but not coarsely modelled : the forehead was full, high, and finely outlined, as she had observed when he raised his hat; and there was a sombre power in his large and luminous eye. His face wore an expression of haughty reserve, and his carriage was dignified. His aristocratic bearing was not belied by his manner of speech, which was courtly if somewhat abrupt.

"Permit me," said he, "to explain my presence here. I have heard that a certain young lady had expressed surprise that I should leave this well in such a state of ruinous neglect; and I came to judge for myself, and to arrange for its proper repair."

"Believe me, sir, I did not impute blame," said Sibylla, with a heightened colour.

"I accept the assurance, and indeed it is not strictly my duty to keep this place in order; for though it lies perhaps within the precincts of the estate, there is right-of-way, and the good people who use the well might not unreasonably be expected to do something for it. The trough, I see, is broken, and no doubt in bad weather the approach is muddy. This plank, too, is but a sorry means of access to the salubrious waters. The matter, in short, shall receive immediate attention."

Sibylla bowed, and smiled with a grateful look.

"I am puzzled to conceive who can have

conveyed my random remarks," she said, half - interrogatively. " I fear they must have been exaggerated in the process of transmission."

" Your remarks made a little circuit thus : they travelled from the manse to the school-house, where lives an unsparing critic of the nobility; thence to the inn, there being, people say, subterranean means of communication between the two places—I speak, of course, metaphorically ; then they travelled to me, Mr Simpson being a tenant of mine. How far they have been coloured or swelled in volume after passing through these several channels I know not, nor does it matter, for any one who looks upon Miss Gordon will acquit her of any ungentle expression of opinion."

" It is evident I must be more careful in the future," said Sibylla, with a look of vexation.

" Pray do not bestow a thought upon such a trifle," said Lord. Wimpole. " In a small place like this the origination of ideas is a slow process, and the good folks are glad to borrow the casually expressed opinions of their betters, as the destitute wear second-hand clothes. Well, well, 'tant de bruit pour une omelette'! Mr Gordon has not yet found time to do me the honour of a call——"

"He mentioned that matter this very morning," interposed Sibylla, hastily.

Lord Wimpole bowed.

"I shall be delighted to see him at his convenience. And now, I shall not further intrude. I presume your ship is refitting, Mr Gordon?"

"Yes, sir; it has been a good deal battered about, but we expect to be in proper trim in the course of a few weeks."

"Well, I wish you a full share of glory and prize-money."

"Thank you," said Walter, drily, who thought this a somewhat patronising re-mark.

Then, after the exchange of ceremonious salutations, Lord Wimpole took his leave.

The brother and sister were silent for a few minutes, and then Walter said—

"I dislike the fellow. His very courtesy is offensive ; it is so elaborately ironical."

"I think you exaggerate, Walter," said Sibylla, mildly. "And confess that it was thoughtful of him to act upon a casual remark of mine. It was neighbourly and kind."

"All depends upon the motive," said Walter, with a sombre look. "As Mr Prosser would say, I fear the Danai even when bringing gifts."

"Well, 'tis no matter," was his sister's reply.

But they were silent and preoccupied during their walk home.

CHAPTER V.

ANDREW VISITS HIS AUNT JANE.

IT was Mr Prosser's habit every Wednesday afternoon (Wednesdays and Saturdays being half-holidays) to make an excursion, from which he did not return till some time during the early hours of Thursday morning. Interrogated on the subject, he was accustomed to explain that he had a relative in Dundee—his Aunt Jane—who was in indifferent health, and whom he helped to make up her books, for she kept a chandler's shop. People, however, were wont to shake their heads dubiously when discussing the matter, and though they could not affirm that Aunt Jane was an apocryphal personage, for one or two of the Fownie folks had hunted up her shop, and had even self-sacrificingly bought candles from her, nevertheless it was surmised either that some female, younger and more attractive than Aunt Jane, was the occasion of these toilsome pilgrimages—who would walk fourteen miles to see an aunt?—or that Andrew was a member of a secret political club, and that Aunt Jane was but a colourable pretext and a sort of friendly flag to mask clandestine commerce and political piracy. But Prosser was not deterred from continuing his habit by these insinuations and suspicions, for he had a stiff sinew in his neck, and had advanced notions of civil liberty. Occasionally, instead of walking the distance, he went to Dundee by sea, accomplishing the journey in a lug-sailed boat obligingly lent him by Simpson, the worthy landlord of the Anchor Inn. "Lent" is, however, hardly the proper word, for in order to requite the obligation, Prosser insisted upon receiving Bell as a free pupil. Great, then, was the astonishment of the good folks of Fownie (for such a village is like a glass hive, the movements of every

member of the community being watched
with close scrutiny), when, one fine Wednesday afternoon, Mr Prosser and Simpson were
seen to embark together in the lug-sailed
boat.   Moreover, Simpson was habited in
an unwonted style.   Instead of his broad
Scots bonnet, which was as well known
as his red shock of hair, he wore a three-
cornered hat, somewhat greasy and battered
indeed, and limp in the flaps, but still
a head - gear arresting attention ; he had
also donned a faded blue coat with brass
buttons ; and, instead of his long well-oiled
boots reaching above the knee, he wore
buckled shoes.   His rubicund face, sur-
rounded by its nimbus of red hair, sleeked,
however, for the occasion, was charged
with an expression of solemn importance,
a little spoiled by the somewhat uneasy
glances of his twinkling and fugitive grey
eyes.

A crowd of loungers on the beach had
gathered to witness the departure of the
strangely assorted pair.

" What's in the wind the day, Tam ? "

asked one, translating into speech the thoughts of all.

"I'm ganging to see a writer," was the reply, uttered in a studied drawl.

"Wae's me!" said another, with mock concern. "That's serious. You'll be making your will, I'se warrant."

"I'll no' leave you anything, Sandy," was the reply, which was received with general laughter.

"How's your Aunt Jane, Mr Prosser?" asked another, with an air of polite inquiry and a circular wink.

"I'll tell her you were speerin' for her, William," said Andrew, coolly; "and she'll maybe give you a dozen farthing dips and a horn lantern to light you when you're stoicherin' hame o' nights."

This allusion to the inquirer's convivial habits raised a laugh at his expense; and the further proceedings of the two men were watched in silence.

The boat was pushed off, the lug-sail hoisted, and in a few minutes the little vessel was skimming along, its progress being attentively watched by the loungers on the shore, till its dwindling outlines diverted their speculation to the chances of the weather.

The wind was steady, and Andrew, who was seated forward, opened conversation with his companion.

" Mind you, Simpson, this is a serious matter, and I dinna want to bind an unwilling victim to the horns of the altar. If at the last moment ye take the rue, say so, and I'll bear nae grudge. Are ye convinced?"

" Ay, I'm convinced," was the gruff reply. " It's a poor Government when the Pert Polly has to play at hide-and-seek with the revenue cutters. I'm for freedom in a' things, in trade particularly. So ye may ding doon the Government as soon as ye like; but I draw the line at the Kirk, Andrew. Ye maunna ding doon the Kirk. I dinna believe in the worship of Reason. Reason is but a farthing dip (as ye were saying to that bletherin' idiot) in matters of eternity. Could Reason have given us a Bible?—answer me that."

"Ye're a fine theologian, Simpson, I ken that, especially when ye hae spirits in the hold," rejoined Andrew, caustically. "But this is a political matter. Leave the Kirk alane; it doesna need you for a buttress or a stoop,—stowps are queer stoops for a Kirk, if ye'll excuse the remark. Tell me, have you got liberty?"

"D—d little!" was the sententious reply.

"Have I got liberty? Why, I canna scrape innocent catgut but they find treason in it. As for freedom of speech or freedom of printing, they simply dinna exist. Oh, Georgius Rex! 'quousque tandem abutere nostra patientia?'"

"Slack aft the sheet, Mr Prosser, a wee bit," said Simpson, who felt that he must assert his nautical superiority when Latin was brought on board.

After a sail of nearly three hours, our voyagers reached Dundee. Proceeding some distance up the Nethergate, Andrew stopped at a low-browed shop and pushed open a half-door, which gave notice of their entrance by setting a bell in clangorous motion. A tall gaunt woman emerged from an inner apartment, and greeted Andrew with a wry smile.

" How are ye, auntie ? " he asked, and then hastily introduced his companion, lest his inquiry should lead to a minute description of her bodily condition.

" Glad to see you, Mr Simpson. Ye look fine and hearty. I wish I was the same. But I'm sair hadden doon wi' a hoast. It is a wearing and a wearying thing a hoast. At night whiles I canna get a wink o' sleep——"

" How's your rheumatism, auntie ? " interposed Andrew, anxious for a change of prolixity.

" Powerful bad, Andrew," replied Aunt Jane, with a doleful shake of the head. " My knee feels whiles as if somebody was boring red-hot needles into it."

" I ken," said Simpson, cordially, for nothing breeds friendship like the comparison of ailments. " You should try hot vomitations,—no that I think muckle o' hot water by itsel'."

" How's business ? " asked Andrew, hastily.

"I dinna ken," said Aunt Jane, dolefully. "It doesna come near my doors. It's the wars that's ruining everything."

"No *your* trade, auntie, for when there's a great victory—and how do the puir French folk manage to exist at all when they are being constantly beaten? unless they are like women, dogs, and the sandal-tree, 'the more they be beaten, the better they be'— when there's a victory, there's an illumination, and your stock melts away fast enough."

"Ay, and the folks gang to their beds in the dark for a fortnight afterhin. I get nae benefit from your ile-luminations. It's a puir trade, and the smell o' the tallow gets round my heart."

"Ye should take a thimblefu' o' cognac now and then," said Simpson.

"Nae doot," was the dejected reply, "but it's dear."

Simpson coughed, and cleared his throat.

"I hae a friend," said he, with a vague sweep of his hand, "who gets it cheap. If you'll accept a bottle——"

" That will I," said Aunt Jane, with alacrity,
" and you'll get a widow's blessing."

" Now, we must be off, auntie," said
Andrew, who was fidgeting about impatiently.

" Ay, ay, Andrew ; I never get mair than
just a glisk o' ye. Dinna mind me,—I'm
only a lone widow."

" We'll be back again in two or three
hours," said Andrew, " and we might take
a rizzered haddie, or something of that sort."

" Ay, ay," said Aunt Jane, resignedly.

The two men advanced for some distance
up the street, and then Andrew, after a
swift exploring glance, turned hastily into
a close, and ascended the stairs at its farther
extremity. He stopped at the first landing
and gave three interspaced knocks at a low
door. A small slide closing a spy-hole, or
" speer," as it was sometimes called, was
shot to one side, and after the visitors had
been apparently reconnoitred, a lean forefinger, not particularly clean, and with an
ebony frame round the nail, was thrust out.
Andrew placed his own forefinger over it

crosswise, and immediately thereafter the door was unbolted, thrown open, and as instantly closed when the two men had entered. A strangely attired figure met Simpson's astonished gaze. A tall man stood before him in the lobby, holding a candlestick in his left hand. A dingy white tunic, the breast of which was emblazoned with a large red cross made of silk, descended to his ankles, and his head was adorned with a Phrygian cap.

"Welcome, Athanasius," he said to Andrew, solemnly. "Take off your shoes, stranger," he added, turning to Simpson with an imposing gesture of command.

Simpson dutifully obeyed, and through two large holes in his stockings displayed a pair of blushing heels.

The three men then entered a largish apartment, in which about a score of men were seated on benches covered with red baize. They were all, like the personage who had opened the door, habited in white tunics, only the red crosses upon their breasts were of smaller dimensions. On

Andrew and Simpson entering, all rose, and a murmur of "Welcome, Athanasius," passed round the room.

After some low-voiced conversation, the tall man, who was evidently the master of ceremonies, rose and said solemnly—

"The initiation will now take place."

He bent down and traced with chalk a triangle upon the wooden floor. Then addressing Simpson curtly, he said, "Stranger, stand within." Simpson did so, with a sheepish and somewhat anxious look, glancing round in search of Andrew, who, however, had retired to a side-room in order to don his white robe and red cap.

When Andrew had re-entered the room, and the Chapter had been constituted, the master of ceremonies took his stand upon a small platform opposite the triangularly marked space and addressed Simpson in tones of exaggerated solemnity—

"Stranger, our Brother Athanasius has reported that you wish to become a member of the Grand Associated Order of Knight-Templars. Is that so?"

Simpson replied in the affirmative.

"Brothers Athanasius and Bernardus, blindfold him."

This was done, and Brother Bernardus, drawing a pistol out of his pocket, fired it off close to Simpson's ear. If this was an experiment to test the steadiness of his nerves, the results were satisfactory, for Simpson merely started, and, pulling off the bandage round his brows, looked round with a threatening scowl.

"I shall now explain the ceremonies and symbols of your initiation," said the officiating Templar, calmly ignoring Simpson's displeasure. "Take off your coat. This is to signify that you are to strip off the rags and tatters of your present superstitions, religious and political; and in future you will wear in these assemblies, or Chapters, as we prefer to call them, the white robe, emblem of our pure and elevated faith, adorned with the red cross, which is the symbol of the crusade we wage against political and social error."

Simpson was now led forward to a table

on which stood a small holly-tree, set in
an earthenware pot and garnished with a
number of small red candles, which were
now lighted.

"This," said the Chief Templar, "is the
Burning Bush. The people are in Egyptian
bondage, and we are to lead them forth
into the Land of Liberty. Each member
of the Order is a Moses, who has renounced
allegiance to Pharaoh."

This remark was greeted with subdued
applause.

Simpson was now led up to a carpet
suspended on a cord across the room.

"This is the veil of the Temple," continued the orator, "which, as you see, is
rent from top to bottom. Pass through,
with head erect."

Simpson obeyed.

"This implies," resumed the interpreter,
"that the old dispensation is annulled, that
the Law is cancelled, and the Liberty of
the Gospel of Humanity achieved."

After a pause, Simpson was now conducted
to a table on which was an object concealed

beneath a white cloth, which being removed, disclosed to view a human skull filled with a red liquid.

"All Sacraments are consecrated with blood," continued the officiating Templar. "Drink."

"That I winna," exclaimed Simpson, growing pale, and with a grimace of disgust.

This emphatic refusal, which he had reinforced with an oath, provoked a burst of indignation from the assembled knights. But Andrew whispered something in Simpson's ear, who muttered discontentedly, "Ye might hae told me it was claret, though I would hae preferred whisky."

"Silence!" said the Chief Templar, in solemn rebuke. "Drink. This liquor is the symbol of the blood which must be shed before liberty is attained, and this skull is the emblem of Death, for Death is the parent of Life: the seed must die before the new plant germinates. The chosen People must exterminate the Canaanites. Drink!"

Simpson gingerly lifted the skull, and

swallowed a mouthful with a very wry face.

A sword was now put into his hand.

" With this sword," the gruesome personage continued, " you will attack the enemies of our Order and defend your brethren in all circumstances, even in case of murder or treason, and you will not disclose the secrets of the Order under pain of death, and you will, if so commanded by the Chapter, use the sword or other mortal weapons, whereof this sword is the comprehensive expression, without hesitation or remorse.   Kneel !"

Simpson obeyed with a look of trepidation, and the Chief Templar, dipping the point of the sword into the liquor contained by the skull, said—

" I name thee Brother Bonifacius, in the name of Liberty, Fraternity, and Equality."

Having touched Simpson on the shoulder with the sword, he added, " Rise, Brother Bonifacius, your initiation is complete.   Go to the vestry and don the white robe."

The tedious and fantastic ceremony being

ended, the business of the Chapter began, and was not concluded till nearly ten o'clock, by which time Brother Bonifacius was nodding sleepily in his seat, little disturbed by the strife of tongues which raged without intermission, and which threatened at times to culminate in blows; for the liberty of speech professed and practised by each Knight-Templar was balanced by an equal liberty to knock down a brother Templar for expressing uncongenial sentiments.

At last the meeting broke up, and Andrew with his associate returned to Aunt Jane's abode. Having partaken of refreshment, they proceeded to the harbour, and about midnight set sail for Fownie, where they safely landed after a somewhat rough passage, during which Simpson occasionally revived his spirits by application to a whisky-flask.

His last words as he parted from Andrew were uttered in a husky whisper—

"Ding doon the Government if ye like, but I draw the line at the Kirk. 'Her very dust to me is dear.'"

At this point he showed emotion, and Andrew said impatiently—

" Hoots awa ! ye're greetin' fou, Simpson. But, mind, a close mouth about this night's proceedings, or ye might get tapped for— whisky-and-water."

And with a significant gesture he strode off towards the schoolhouse.

Simpson stared after him for a while with tipsy gravity, and then, with a derisive snap of his fingers, stumbled off towards the inn, muttering to himself.

CHAPTER VI.

LORD WIMPOLE HAS A TALK WITH SIBYLLA.

In those stirring and heroic days of which we write, life resembled a bustling farce, or a tragedy with swiftly succeeding episodes of terror and disaster. Life was adventurous because the living sought adventure, and squandered their vitality royally by land and sea, supporting their fine extravagance on post-obits of glory. But even then the action flagged at times, and the spectators yawned at stretches of prosy commonplace. Even good Homer nods occasionally, and the epic of humanity, when George the Third was king, grew now and then mortally dull. Or, to use a figure more suited to those days, when Britain was at once the Rome and the Carthage of

Europe, and wielded no doubtful sovereignty of the seas, the peaceful trade-winds succeeded the " roaring Forties."

In Fownie things had settled into dull placidity. Mr Prosser taught the village school with quiet assiduity, and visited his Aunt Jane with exemplary regularity ; Simpson landed his cargoes, and made money fast ; Gillespie's zeal as an excise officer was tempered with bouts of drinking, and his big dog, as well known and as much feared as himself, had gone mad, and had to be shot ; Walter was in the West Indies, varying his activity with attacks of fever—he had Yellow Jack twice, but stopped short each time at the " black vomit "; his sister became month by month more richly beautiful, like some exuberant passion-flower ; Mr Marjoribanks finished his stock of sermons and began them over again, like a barrel-organ with its tunes ; his daughter grew more pensive and reserved ; and Bell emerged into maidenhood. Lord Wimpole had come and gone at frequent intervals, looking as disdainfully saturnine as ever, and now in the spring of 1794 he was installed at Swinton Hall. He had become a regular visitor at Beechgrove, where Mr Gordon always made him heartily welcome. Sibylla's feelings could not be so easily divined. She was invariably courteous; but a certain distant coolness, like wind blowing off snow, played upon the surface of her manner.

It was a pleasant afternoon; and Lord Wimpole had ridden over to see Mr Gordon on a matter of business, some daring cases of poaching having recently occurred. After despatching business, he had been invited to enter the drawing-room, where Sibylla was employed with some tapestry-work as interminable as Penelope's web.

"Sibylla, dear, entertain Lord Wimpole for a short while," said her father; "I have some depositions to receive. Will your lordship excuse me?"

"By all means. But I fear to trouble Miss Gordon."

Sibylla made a deprecating movement with her hand, and invited him to take a seat.

"Near the fire, my lord, for I have observed
that, like myself, you like warmth."

"I am a salamander, if I may speak tropi-
cally," he said, with a smile. "Purgatory
must be very bad to frighten me; and the
priests must do what the Greenland mission-
aries had to do, substitute ice for fire."

"Satirical as usual, my lord. Are you
never in earnest?"

"The most dangerous people in the world
are the earnest ones. They upset thrones
and convulse society. The cynics are the
salt of the earth."

"But progress, Lord Wimpole! Without
the earnest people there would be no
progress."

"I doubt it very much. Your men of
progress are the flies on the carriage-wheel;
they think they are making it go on. They
make indeed *revolutions*," he went on, smiling
at the conceit; "but in reality they and we
are impelled by unseen and inscrutable
forces. Pooh! they are conceited fools, when
they think humanity dances to the jingling
of their bells."

Gazing abstractedly at the blazing billets on the hearth, he sank into a gloomy reverie. Sibylla sat equally silent, with a faint smile on her lips. She inwardly preferred his taciturnity to modish chatter, and there was a nameless charm in this pensive *tête-à-tête*.

" I have sometimes thought," he said, looking up with a smile, " that the Catholic Church, which shows so deep and true a knowledge of human nature, might with advantage have instituted an order of virgin confessors."

" I hardly understand, my lord."

"I beg your pardon. What I mean is this : there should be virgin confessors, to whom a man might confide in solemn secrecy his sins and errors. After all a priest is a man, not much, if at all, better than your average mortal; and while I would scorn to confess to such a man, it would be a great relief for me to tell some saintly maiden what has so often caused me· remorse. Her very ignorance of evil would point the contrast, and disclose the great gulf between purity and guilt. Then how

gently would she reprove, perchance she
might shed a few pitying tears, and with
her keen intuitions she would detect the
latent germ of goodness, and appraise the
force of circumstance, which leads often to
such desperate results. For example, why
should not I confess to you? I know you
well now, and I feel a sense of repose in
your presence which I feel nowhere else ;
why then should I not invoke a sister-spirit
to my aid ? "

"Indeed, my lord, you could not have
a kinder confessor, if I may be so bold :
but I have my illusions, which I do not
wish destroyed ; and I conjecture that as
regards your moral health you are a ' malade
imaginaire.' "

" Ah, Sibylla, Sibylla ! " he said, softly.

The gentle ruefulness of his tone touched
her heart. Her eyes filled with tears, and
the sweet girlishness of her look gave place
to a woman's yearning gaze, as she glanced
at his brooding countenance flickeringly
illumined by the light of the fire.

" Well, well," he said, with an impatient

sigh. "Keep your illusions as long as you can. Some day you will know me, and, I fear, respect me less."

"Never!"

"Fond enthusiast! You impute your own virtues."

"This is strange talk, my lord, and let me end it thus: if ever you are in deep distress, let me know; perhaps I shall instinctively know, and then I shall be your confessor and consoler, if I may, in all sisterly and womanly sincerity."

"A vow! a vow!" he exclaimed. "Rash girl! you know not what you commit yourself to."

"Yes, I know," she replied, nodding her head gently in affirmation. "Is it self-praise to say that I am the genius of sorrow? In my happiest moments — and I have many such — I never forget my future destiny. There is something here tells me" — and she laid her hand upon her heart—"that I shall never be supremely happy till I am supremely miserable. But I feel too that the finest joy, the most pungent ecstasy, is wrung from a bleeding heart. Who can paint the raptures of the Mother of Sorrows?"

They sat silent for a long time, and then he said—

"All this is in the vein of the melancholy Jacques. Let us change the current of our thoughts. Will you sing me 'Santa Lucia'? The last time you sang it, your voice haunted me for days. I cannot myself account for it, but I am passionately fond of music. It is almost the only pleasure I am susceptible of now."

"I shall be delighted," she replied, with glad alacrity.

"Of course with a guitar accompaniment. I like its delicious throbs of sentiment and pathos."

Sibylla was an accomplished musician, and her voice was a rich and sympathetic contralto, so that the simple but beautiful Neapolitan air was exquisitely rendered; and Lord Wimpole's face was almost transfigured as he listened to the melting strains.

"Your name should have been Cecilia,"

he said, when she had finished with a crisp and delicate arpeggio. "Nay, to me it shall be Cecilia. Now, divine Cecilia, let me have 'O Santissima.'"

Her cheeks were flushed, her eyes sparkling with delight.

Fond girl! he played upon her heart as movingly as she upon her guitar. And could he misinterpret the delicate reserve which silently chid his inexplicable silence?

Before she had finished the song, her father had re-entered the room. He held an open letter in his hand, but stood listening till the last lingering cadence had died away.

"A letter from Walter, dear," he said, eagerly. "He is at Plymouth, he says, but won't have time to visit us. The Hecla is revictualling. Listen to this, my lord, and judge of the sort of rapacious villains who provision his Majesty's ships nowadays. But perhaps I detain you."

"Not in the least. Pray proceed," said Lord Wimpole, courteously.

"This is what Walter says," continued

Mr Gordon: " 'The provisions during our
last cruise in the Mediterranean have been
scandalously bad. The salt beef, which we
had to eat so constantly that we all got
scurvy more or less, was at times half putrid.
The "hard-tack" was only soft where there
were maggots and weevils, and we had to
rap each biscuit soundly, to make the abom-
inations drop out. For breakfast we got
burgoo (or porridge), with treacle so called,
for I would prefer to call it muddy syrup,
and you came upon insects in it constantly,
which I think must have died of sheer disgust. The drinking-water, too, had not been
obtained from a pure source; it stank like
bilge-water, and when I drained it through
my pocket-handkerchief I had to hold my
nose (tell Sibylla to think of that when she
uses lavender-water). I had scurvy on the
hands and face; but when we put into Coron
in the Morea we got plenty of raw onions,
which we devoured with more avidity than
if they had been sugar-plums. That soon
cured us. But why have we not a regular
supply of lemons? The fact is, we are pro-

visioned by a set of swindling scamps, who
amass wealth by buying up abominable stuff
for our consumption, and who can afford to
bribe knaves in office to wink at their dis-
honesty.   I am certain that this usage of
our gallant seamen will end in a serious
mutiny some day.   There is much smouldering discontent, and the discipline is in not a
few ships brutally harsh.   I am thankful to
say that the Hecla is fortunate in having an
excellent captain, who is simply adored by all
of us, and who maintains the finest order with
extremely little punishment.   Not that he is
lenient—God bless him!—for he has several
times given me sky-parlour (that is, sent me
to the main-topmast-head, and kept me
there three or four hours, which means
being congealed or carbonadoed according
to the weather).   But no doubt I deserved
it.   I may add that soap has been rather
scarce, and we had often to turn our stockings, &c.   As Tom Harris, our second lieu-
tenant, says jocularly, "One good turn deserves another."   As we put in our stores
in a great hurry, many things were over-

looked ; and we have had much discomfort
in consequence. But there is no use com-
plaining, and with issues so mighty at stake,
we have little reason to be fastidious or
fault-finding. A great deal depends upon
the general sentiment pervading the ship,
and as that is very healthy on board the
Hecla, we laugh our troubles off and make
a jest of them. Tom Harris is great at
this, and has all kinds of nautical similes
for our makeshift contrivances. For example, he was invited one day to dine
with the captain ; but his only presentable
pair of stockings had a hole in the ankle
which he had no time to darn, even if he
had the worsted, which I doubt. So he
wrapped a handkerchief round his ankle, and
gravely informed the captain that he had
barked his shin in going down the companion. This he called " fothering the leak "
(you must understand that fothering is clapping a sail over a hole to keep out the
water). We had several times a lively brush
with the French, but that's all in the way of
business ; besides, they fight fair, and when

they have struck their flag, they are polite and good-natured enough, especially if you know a little of their lingo. What we detest is the privateers and the Algerian pirates, for they are as treacherous as they are cruel. We give them no quarter. A Moorish dance at the end of a yard-arm is the only polite entertainment that suits them.' I am afraid, my lord, that I am grievously abusing your patience. You cannot be expected to be interested as I am by my dear boy's garrulous letter."

"On the contrary, it is quite a pleasure to listen to his fresh impressions. Besides, I was in the navy myself, and can sympathise with his feelings."

"You are very kind to say so. By the way, there is a matter I wish to speak to you about at your leisure; but there is no hurry, and I must not trespass on your courtesy."

"My dear sir, my time is not as well filled as it ought to be, and Beechgrove Hall is not a place one is in haste to leave."

Mr Gordon bowed, with a gratified look.

"Well, as you are so obliging, the matter is this. You need not go away, Sibylla: it interests you even more than me, for mine is only a kind of deputed interest, Mr Marjoribanks having requested me to appeal to Lord Wimpole on the subject. He thinks that Simpson of the Anchor Inn is not treating his niece properly."

Lord Wimpole's brows contracted, and a dusky flush mounted to the very roots of his hair.

"I am afraid I have unwittingly given your lordship offence. But if you will allow me to complete my explanation——"

"Pray, proceed, sir," said Lord Wimpole, abruptly. "Both matter and manner are totally void of offence."

"Mr Marjoribanks conjectures, and my daughter also thinks, that Simpson has the enjoyment of some means or property belonging to his niece, and accruing to her when she comes of age by her father's settlement. Now, if this be so, it is manifest that Miss Bell—so we always call her,

and a more charming girl does not exist—
should receive such an education and such
treatment as befits her future position. She
has, I believe, been well educated at the
village school; for Mr Prosser is an excellent teacher, whatever be his demerits,
on which I am loath to dilate, and he has,
moreover, taken a deep interest in her in
a very chivalrous and unselfish way, as I
am bound to say,—I am afraid I am imi-
tating my son's prolixity. What we think
is, that she should be sent to a genteel ladies'
seminary, to fit her either for her future
position as a lady, or, if that be too san-
guine an expectation, to enable her to earn
her living in a cultivated and respectable
way. She has excellent abilities, and the
most exquisite voice you can imagine : even
my daughter——"

"Avows her inferiority," interposed Sibylla, in a low voice.

"'Tis too great a demand upon my credul-
ity to admit that," said Lord Wimpole, who
had recovered his outward composure.

"At any rate," continued Mr Gordon,

"she is well fitted to adorn any situation in life. Now, my lord, I feel a delicacy in proceeding farther; but Simpson, I believe, is a tenant of yours, and speaks of you in warm terms as having befriended him in earlier days——"

"The babbling sot exaggerates," said Lord Wimpole, with the same heightened colour and contraction of his eyebrows. "He rendered a service to a kinsman of mine, which I have requited in some slight way, particularly in not raising his rent, for he is making a fortune under my nose. I anticipate your request, Mr Gordon. It is that I should interrogate him, and impress upon him that the young lady, whom I have several times seen, and who certainly seems to justify the high opinion which her friends have of her—that I should see she gets justice. Now, my influence with Simpson is no doubt considerable, but whether it would warrant my active interference is questionable."

"I quite perceive that, my lord," said Mr Gordon, who was evidently anxious to drop the subject.

"Nevertheless," continued Lord Wimpole, "the matter shall be looked into, and that speedily. It is certain that Simpson is a hypocritical dog, who sails very near the wind in business matters. But am I to understand"—he went on with a strange, and it seemed angry, sparkle of the eye— "that Miss—that the young lady, for so I may call her, if Miss Gordon is her friend— has menial work to perform, or serves noggins of ale to Simpson's boozing rascals?"

"I think she is well enough treated in these matters," replied Mr Gordon. "Simpson's fault is rather one of omission than commission. Besides, Mrs Simpson is occasionally addicted to intemperance, and—but I need not pursue the subject further. Your lordship sees the situation."

"Clearly, and you may reckon on the fullest exercise of my influence. Though, of course, I cannot guarantee Simpson's concurrence with the views of Miss Bell's friends."

"Of course not, and I hope we are not suggesting an intervention on your part likely to be unpleasant."

"The unpleasantness will have its compensations," said Lord Wimpole, with a courteous bow.

Then, having raised Sibylla's hand to his lips, he bowed to Mr Gordon and withdrew.

Father and daughter were silent for a while after his departure, and then Mr Gordon said, with an inquiring look—

"Well, my dear, and what do you think of him?"

"I don't exactly know what to think," she replied, with a slight blush.

"He seems to like your society; but if his visits have no serious motive, I confess I would rather he discontinued them. Moreover, he seems to me a moody, discontented, and choleric man."

"On the surface, perhaps."

"Pardon the question, my dear, but am I to understand——"

"Pray don't ask me anything, for I cannot answer," said Sibylla, precipitately. "I think that with time he will come to understand his own feelings."

"And what of your own feelings, Sibylla?"

"Ah, dearest papa, if I am ever to be unhappy, it will be through him," and she
clasped her arms round her father's neck.
As she did so he felt a tear fall on his cheek,
while a shuddering sob seemed to convulse
her tender frame. With a look of deep concern, he gently unwound her arms and kissed
her on the brow.

"Do not, at least, Sibylla, cultivate your
own unhappiness," he said, with affectionate
earnestness. "Few men, least of all Lord
Wimpole, are worth a woman's lasting sorrow."

"And few men forbear to inflict it," said
Sibylla, in a broken voice.

CHAPTER VII.

MILLY'S PROFESSION OF FAITH.

On the Saturday evening of this same week, Andrew Prosser, after a simple meal of porridge-and-milk, retired to 'his bedroom and donned his Sunday suit, — for, being precentor at the kirk, he had to arrange for the service of praise on the following day. This suit was somewhat rusty at the seams, though a periodical attempt was made to revive its pristine black by sponging it with ink-and-water. The ruffles of his shirt, too, were considerably frayed at the edges — a defect only to be mitigated by a severe degree of starching. Still, he did not look amiss, for success in wearing a black suit is largely attained by filling it. Mrs Badger,

who was ironing, and had a very inflamed
face and temper in consequence, stared at
him—for he did not usually don his official
coat on such occasions—and remarked with
a sour smile : " A body might think ye had
the wedding-garment on, Andrew, in the
worldly meaning of the word ; for as to the
spiritual meaning, I'm afraid your righteousness is but as filthy rags."

" Ay, ay," said Andrew ; " ye are fond o'
giving me ' the sincere milk of the word,'
but it's aye lippered, I find.   Ye needna bide
up for me ; I'm gangin' to the minister's."

" Ye keep braw hours when ye gang there,"
rejoined Mrs Badger. " If it was a tavern,
a body wouldna wonder ; but I'll wad a
guinea—if it wasna sinful to bet—that even
Simpson is in his bed when the minister is
scraping away on his big fiddle and drinking
toddy.   Wae's me for the Kirk of Scotland ;
it's a kennel for dumb dogs that will not
bark."

" They dinna snarl, at any rate," said
Andrew, goaded to indignation. " I' faith,
if ye will use such a comparison, the Kirk is

like a big sonsy Newfoundland with a lot o'
terriers and mongrel curs barking at its
heels.   But it disna fash itself, and it doesna
need, for a' these tykes are ower busy worry-
ing ane anither to do *it* any harm."

" Ye're a queer mixture, Andrew," said Mrs
Badger, with mild sarcasm.   " Ye dinna believe in kings, and yet King George is head
o' the Kirk as by law established.   What
would the Kirk be without the King ? "

" Hoots, Mrs Badger," exclaimed Andrew,
wincing a little, "it's no' the king's image
and superscription that makes a gold guinea
valuable ; it's the worth of the metal.   But
I have no time to be claverin' here.   Guid
nicht."

" Guid nicht, Andrew," said Mrs Badger, as
solemnly as if she were bidding him a last
farewell with serious doubts as to his ulti-
mate destination.

Andrew made his way towards the manse
in a very dejected state of mind.   He was
deeply but hopelessly in love, and he was
very poor.   His statutory salary was £6, 11s.
1⅓d. ('tis well to be accurate), and his fees

amounted to £9, not including what he got for teaching Latin, which was 12 shillings per annum for each pupil. His office as session-clerk brought him £2. Then he got a few presents from his pupils at Candlemas by ancient prescription. In addition, there were a few "perquisites." Every school in those days that wished to maintain its reputation had a main of cocks; the lads must have their cock-pit, to imbibe by force of imitation a staunch and dauntless spirit, which, alas! often received its quietus in another kind of cock-pit. The schoolmaster had a right to the cocks that were killed, as also to the *fugies*—to wit, those fowls which showed a recreant and craven disposition, and fled from the arena. Summing up every source of emolument, his income may have amounted to £25, with free house and garden. Such was the pecuniary position of schoolmasters a century ago. Small wonder, then, if Andrew was depressed, with love and poverty at ceaseless war.

On reaching the manse, Andrew was ushered by Kirstie — the elderly serving-

woman—into the little sitting-room, where
he found Mrs Marjoribanks and her daughter
quietly sewing.

Mrs Marjoribanks was a genteel little
lady, who looked almost as youthful as her
daughter, so fresh and fair was her complexion and so bright her eyes. Formidable
eyes they were, keen as well as bright,
and with a half-mocking, half-good-natured
gleam in them. Her genially satirical smile
disclosed tiny teeth in excellent preserva-
tion, which promised many a bite yet at
the world's apple. Her manner was one
of somewhat aggressive frankness, and
Andrew stood greatly in awe of her, as
big men do of little ladies, who, it is well
known, are the most charming tyrants in
the world.

" Good evening, Andrew," she said, patron-
isingly. " The minister is out visiting. A
thing they call influenza is very common
just now. We used to call it a catarrh or a
feverish cold ; but the doctors like to invent
new names for maladies they cannot cure.
Will you take a seat ? "

Andrew did so, and then addressed the younger lady—

"I hope I see you well, Miss Marjoribanks?"

"Quite well, I thank you, Mr Prosser."

"You are not 'quite well, I thank you,' my dear," said Mrs Marjoribanks, tartly. "You mope in the house too much. Have you been out to-day?"

"No, mamma."

"Then take Mr Prosser into the garden and show him our Gloire de Dijon roses."

"Very well, mamma," was the dutiful reply, as Miss Marjoribanks rose slowly and reluctantly from her seat, and led the way to the garden. Both of the young people seemed embarrassed and ill at ease.

"Miss Marjoribanks, we schoolmasters are an unhappy body of men," said Andrew, as he softly stroked the petals of a full-blown rose.

"You have many troubles and annoyances, doubtless,—stupid or refractory children, unreasonable parents— "

"Well, I did not exactly mean that. If a

child is stupid, well, nature meant it to be so, and you can't make a silk purse out of a sow's ear, as the proverb says. As for refractory children, the rod is a wholesome corrective; and when parents are troublesome, you can shut the door in their face. But one thing we schoolmasters can't do—we can't keep the wolf from the door. I am a very poor man, Miss Marjoribanks."

"I hope it will not be always so, for your sake."

He shook his head.

" Why, I could make more in a month by smuggling than in half a year by the exercise of my vocation, for I can lay aloft in a gale of wind, splice a rope, fish a spar, or take my trick at the wheel with the best of them."

" The money so made would be the price of degradation, Mr Prosser," said Miss Marjoribanks, earnestly.

" Do not imagine that I regret my poverty, save for one reason," he said, huskily.

He took her hand and pressed it to his lips before she could prevent the impulsive action.

" Ah, Miss Marjoribanks, to know you, to love you with every fibre of my poor heart, and yet to feel that my poverty is an impassable barrier—that is misery indeed."

His emotion was too sincere not to touch her heart. Her cheeks were glowing with maidenly embarrassment, but there was a gentle look in her eyes, and her lips trembled as she said—

" You are, I fear, prone to exaggeration and extremes, Mr Prosser. I have simple wishes and simple needs, and I do not fear poverty — if I were sure of undivided affection."

" Undivided ! " he repeated, in a tone of reproachful astonishment. " You are the only woman I have ever loved, or ever will love."

" Let us be perfectly frank with one another," she said, after a pause, during which she manifestly struggled with her emotion. " I do not speak of any other woman. I believe—yes, I will say the word which is to me a sacred one—I believe you love me truly——"

" Yes, ever since you were my pupil. Ah, these were happy days, when I was sure of seeing you every morning, coming in with your gentle smile ; you were fourteen or fifteen then——"

" I was a spoiled pupil, I fear," she said, with a tearful smile. " And I often wondered why your voice was so different when you spoke to me. But still, Mr Prosser, I have a rival."

" I hardly understand," he stammered.

" I think you do," she rejoined. " My rival is Politics, or shall I say—Conspiracy ? Ah, Mr Prosser, if you knew how fervently I wish you would renounce such vain and utopian schemes—not to call them criminal and seditious,—if you knew how often I lie awake at night, thinking, thinking, and— why should I conceal it ? — praying for you——"

She stopped, overpowered by grief.

" Heaven bless you, dear, dear Milly," he said, in a choking voice.

" I am a child," she gasped, impatiently brushing away her tears. " It is a privilege to be loved—often it is woman's only privilege—and I would give my heart freely to a good man's keeping, but I must feel that it would be safe there."

" You doubt me ? "

" I do," she replied, tremulously, but yet firmly. " My notions are doubtless old-fashioned, but there are three names I revere—God, the Church, and the King. I cannot argue with you. My feelings go deeper than any reason. I wish no Goddess of Reason instead of a blessed Heavenly Father—to His name be praise !—I wish no bloodthirsty Dictator instead of our good old King; no declaration of the Rights of Man instead of the Gospel. The shadow of the Church fell upon my cradle ; may it fall upon my grave ! I could never link my hand with any man, if I thought he was a disloyal subject."

" You forget the tyranny and oppression to which we are subjected," said Andrew; in a low voice.

" The Government cannot palter with treason when the very existence of the

kingdom is at stake. But I will not argue.
Those who are not satisfied with their
country at such a crisis should leave it.
Freedom will come when we are able to
enjoy it. I have not read as much as you
have, perhaps fortunately for me ; but I believe that it has been devotion, truth, self-
sacrifice, and obedience that have made
Britain great,—not charters, declarations,
constitutions, spun like cobwebs in the
brains of lawyers' clerks and pamphle-
teers."

To say that Andrew was astonished by
this fervent language is but a weak expression. Miss Marjoribanks was so habit-
ually calm and self-restrained, that her deep
and glowing earnestness was a revelation.
Her soft and gracious beauty was transfigured, her eyes were brighter, her bearing
more noble, and her voice, usually so mild,
was rich and vibrating. And as indignant
sincerity almost compels conviction, Andrew
felt a sense of meanness and discomfiture
new to him. He involuntarily contrasted
this passionate earnestness with the turgid

eloquence of the Knight - Templars, this
warm devotion with their envenomed hate.

"Believe me, Miss Marjoribanks," he said,
humbly, "my motives are good."

"I know that, and it makes me all the
sadder. Do you think I would have spoken
so to a base revolutionary?"

"It adds to my misery that you condemn
me," he went on. "The times are all out of
joint; I know not why I should continue to
live."

"I would implore you to do nothing rash
or desperate," she said, with an anxious look.
"Both my convictions and my feelings are
indeed unchangeable—do not forget that;
and you have perchance much suffering before you. But do not think yourself utterly
forsaken. I shall never forget you, though
I deplore your errors. And I am sure you
will abandon your present opinions after
fuller knowledge and experience. Is it presumptuous to say so? So true a nature as
yours is cannot for long persist in such unworthy courses. And now we shall speak
no more of this. It is inexpressibly painful

to me; my health is not very strong just now, and I cannot bear much agitation. It will not seem strange to you if you seldom see me."

He covered his eyes with his hand to hide the tears that filled them.

" I shall leave you now," she added. " You might wait here till papa joins you. Farewell."

She held out her hand, which he took and pressed to his lips.

" Farewell ! " he repeated. " Think of me as kindly as you can."

Her only reply was a stifled sob, as she swiftly withdrew.

Not long after Mr Marjoribanks entered the garden. His manner was constrained, and his look clouded.

" I hear strange things of you, Andrew," he said, a little hesitatingly, after some general conversation. " Bear in mind that the whole country just now is an ear of Dionysius. I would not that you contribute your whisper, for it will reach the tyrant's ear. We understand each other. Set it down that few causes are worthy of martyrdom. I am a Moderate; I don't much believe in enthusiasm of any kind, unless it be musical enthusiasm, which is, after all, half sensual. If we could preserve those moods which a starry night inspires, we would take a saner view of the world and ourselves. What are we in the stream of existence? 'Tis our vanity that drapes us in importance. How vain our hopes and our ambitions, how ephemeral our joys! So deeply is Christianity pervaded with this feeling, that it is ever looking forward beyond this scene of being."

"It is deeply true," said Andrew, with a sombre look. "But early Christianity taught a different lesson from what you are reading me."

"Yes; because the early Christians despised this world, and looked perpetually forward to a better. But that was pious despair, excusable perhaps in the deplorable state of Roman society. For a half-way house this world is a comfortable place enough, and I'll e'en take mine ease in

mine inn. Christianity was never meant
to make us querulous, still less seditious.
'Render unto Cæsar the things that are
Cæsar's.' What means this homily, Andrew? This, namely : that you should not
fash your thumb about the State. It's bad
enough, no doubt, but it is better than
anarchy. Our king is not a Solon or a
Solomon ; he is safer as he is. A clever
king is as dangerous — as a clever wife !
Tyranny, my dear lad ! Wait till you are
married, and then perhaps you will admit
that a certain degree of tyranny is not a
bad thing. Would I ever change my damp
clothes when I come home if my good lady
did not compel me ? And so a cohort of
diseases, as friend Horace says, has been
put to flight. Even Mrs Badger has her
use, and is doubtless as salutary as a mus-
tard-plaster."

Andrew could not help joining, though
ruefully, in the minister's laugh.

"The conclusion of the whole matter is
—let the world wag ! I have observed that
very often a good old clock does not go

so well after it has been cleaned and re-
paired as it did before. As for charters
and declarations, they are good for lining
trunks, but for nothing else that I can see :
I would not give a Gavotte of Rameau
for the whole of them. My advice, then,
is the Pythagorean maxim : 'Stir not the
fire with the sword.' Are you coming in ? "

But Andrew dejectedly declined, and bade
his friend adieu.

CHAPTER VIII.

BELL VISITS SWINTON HALL.

LORD WIMPOLE was speaking in moderation
when he said that he had seen Bell several
times. He had met her indeed so frequently
during his recent visits to Fownie, that a
young lady with a nice perception of amatory
omens would have refused to recognise hap-
hazard as responsible for these encounters.
Sometimes he arrived at Beechgrove Hall
when she was there, and she had to curtsey
to him before she withdrew. At other times
he was coming up the avenue as she was
going down, or the reverse. And now and
then she met him on the road to Fownie.
On the first few occasions her instincts had
warned her that he regarded her with a

latent antipathy; and when he saluted her with frigid formality, she had seemed to discern a sour and rancorous scorn in his look— at least that was her impression, and women, like other domestic creatures subject to the caprices of man, have keen perceptions.

But the wind had veered into a more genial quarter. He seemed now to be glad to see her. His was one of those wintry countenances which a smile instantly illumines; and when he beheld her approaching, his face at once lost its sombre and repellent look, and his movements became more buoyant. And as those smile most winningly who smile most rarely, this spontaneous irradiation of feature affected her with a strange feeling of delight, which hovered over an abashed dismay.

What can be more thrillingly sweet to a young maid than the homage of a mature man? For if he has been during his previous life insensible to feminine attractions, *she* has mounted the glacis of his well-guarded heart, and if he be *blasé*, she has roused him from his lethargy of feeling.

Bell would not indeed have confessed even to herself that she loved him ; most probably she did not : but perhaps love was beginning to crystallise in her heart,—a sudden shock might determine the cohesion of feeling. Meanwhile her deportment towards him was one of simple dignity.   Those were the days of Evelinas and Camillas, when the " tender passion" was associated with modish affectations, with blushes, tremors, palpitations, vapours, with downcast looks and embarrassed silences, and all the sweet distress of love's captives.   Perhaps, as she curtseyed and then passed on with the blush of a milkmaid and the port of a princess, she offered a pleasing contrast to the young ladies whom he encountered in fashionable society.

Bell had read two or three novels of the period, and knew that all gentlemen may roughly be referred to one of three categories : first, the Fop, who was obtrusive but not dangerous ; second, the Rake, who was both obtrusive and dangerous, and who practised abduction and seduction ; and third, the Lover, who was neither obtrusive nor dangerous, and who, after a series of polite encounters at operas, balls, and ridottos, finally fell on his knees before the object of his respectful adoration and confessed his flame.

Now, Lord Wimpole was not a fop, though always studiously correct in his attire. He did not seem to be a rake, for his bearing was uniformly respectful. But how could he be a lover? That was impossible, for was he not on a dizzy social height above her? He must belong to an unknown category, and in this shadowy limbo she wisely resolved to leave him. Nevertheless, his smile made her heart beat tumultuously.

Then, again, he was almost Sibylla's lover, and it would be treason to friendship even to think of him except as of a gracious personality at an almost immeasurable distance.

Her feelings and fortitude, however, were destined to be put to the proof. For, a couple of days after Lord Wimpole's last visit to Beechgrove Hall, Simpson entered the little parlour where she was seated sewing, and said to her—

"Busk yourself up a bit, my lassie. I'm gangin' with you to Swinton Hall on business."

"With me, uncle?" asked Bell, looking aghast.

"Yes, and ye needna look sae carfuffled : he'll no eat you."

"But what business?"

"Ask nae questions, and I'll tell nae lees —no that I would ever imitate the prophet Ananias."

"I do not wish to meet Lord Wimpole," said Bell, tremulously.

"Hoots! he's auld enough to be your father, wellnigh."

"I don't consider him old," protested Bell.

"I didna say he had ae foot in the grave, did I? But he can look ower his shouther at his youth, for a' that. And as to his reputation — 'gie a dog an ill name' : I ken that by my ain experience. I dinna say he has been a saint,—ye canna keep a man in a glass case ; and, as far as I hae observed, the guid men are either fushionless or hypocritical. The best o' men 'lie among the pots' whiles; but I'll uphaud him for a true gentleman. Sae, gae and pit on your braws. See that ye dinna gang wi' clouted shoon like the Gibeonites, when they went to — where did they gang? Maybe Jabesh - Gilead. Ye like braw things, so that's nae trial."

Bell accordingly made ready with some trepidation to accompany Simpson, who had donned his best suit, and, as attire reacts upon the mind and induces a metaphysical conformity, looked solemn, not to say Sabbatical or funereal.

A walk of a mile took them to the lodge-gate of Swinton Hall. A broad avenue of elms led up to a circular open space in front of the house, which consisted of a large *corps de logis* flanked with massive square wings. The roof was flat and crenelated, and a stone portico ran the entire length of the main building.

A civil elderly woman ushered the two visitors into the library, where they found Lord Wimpole reading. He rose and greeted them with the winning courtesy which in a

man of such a stern and haughty bearing
had all the impressive effect of an agreeable
surprise.   After the exchange of some formal
remarks, he said to Simpson—

"Now, sir, I have some matters to discuss
with your niece, as I informed you; and I
shall beg her to accompany me to the with-
drawing-room for a short time.   Meanwhile,
make yourself at home.   There are various
liquors on the table at your service, and
there are numerous books of divinity — I
know your tastes in both directions.   The
only book pertaining to that class which I
have ever looked into is Jonathan Edwards
on the Will, wherein he proves irrefragably
—in my poor judgment—that we have no
freedom of the will at all, but are always
the slaves of the strongest motive.   It is,
I think, a sound, and sometimes a consola-
tory, doctrine.   You can test it practically,
Simpson, by observing which proves to be
the strongest motive on the present occasion
—rum, whisky, or divinity."

"My lord, knowledge puffeth up," said
Simpson, "so I'll try the whisky."

"Very good. Now, Miss Bell, may I request you to honour me with a short interview on a somewhat important matter ? "

She acquiesced with a curtsey, and he preceded her up a broad stone staircase to the first landing. The walls of this staircase were hung with several dusky oil-paintings, and he paused in his ascent to point them out and comment upon them. He probably wished to divert her attention from the embarrassing novelty of her situation.

"Here is a 'Cain and Abel,' said to be by Giorgione. The treatment is somewhat original. Cain has just slain his brother, and is stooping over a pool to wash his blood-stained hands; he sees in the water the reflection of his face and the divinely imprinted stigma of guilt upon his forehead, and shrinks back in horror, not of his crime, but of the indelible mark which he is doomed to wear.

"This is a 'Fall of the Angels' by a Dutch artist—a mere delirium tremens in pigments. It is to be noticed that the Christian, or perhaps I should rather say the Biblical, mythology has not the repose, the grace, or the dignity of the Greek. Compare a demon with a faun, and you have the difference in a nut-shell. And it all comes to this, that the Hebrews had no humour. — But I must not detain you longer over these paintings."

The withdrawing - room into which he introduced the young girl was a spacious apartment, the furniture of which, though old-fashioned, seemed to Bell's unaccustomed eyes sumptuously magnificent. Lord Wimpole, however, noted with involuntary interest that she did not seem out of place amid the somewhat faded splendour of the room. She was manifestly embarrassed, but showed no sign of awkwardness; and the high-bred refinement of her look and bearing seemed to suit the richness of the apartment. He placed a seat for her beside one of the tall windows, and then sat down at some distance.

" Now, Miss Bell — you will permit me thus to address you, I hope — I have no doubt you have often felt the disharmony of your present surroundings. You have been revolted by the drunkenness, the sordid cupidity, the reckless language, which belong to a common tavern. Moreover, Simpson, though in some respects a meritorious man, is underbred, and Mrs Simpson—pray excuse my plain speaking—is a very unsuitable guardian for a young maiden like you."

"She has always been very kind to me, and I regard her with much affection," said Bell, in a low tone.

"I do not doubt it. Nevertheless, the Anchor Inn is no place for you. Have you formed any plans for the future?"

"I have thought at times of being a lady's-maid," said Bell, with a vivid blush.

Lord Wimpole's face, as if sympathetically, became suffused with a dark crimson, and he cast down his eyes.

"Nay, nay, it will not do," he replied, energetically. "In the first place, I know not if forced submission to a fine lady's whims and fits of spleen would be less galling than your present situation. In the next place, if you will excuse me, you are too beautiful. Your mistress would be jealous of you ; and you would be pestered with the attention of fops and dandies, who think a pretty abigail fair game. I wound your delicacy by these remarks, but the truth must be faced. No, no; you must dismiss that idea. Let me propose another plan. Mr Simpson at one time did me an important service, which I have endeavoured, though inadequately, to requite. Now, I wish to redress the balance of obligation, and I propose the following arrangement— namely, that you should go for a year or two to a ladies' seminary or boarding-school, so as to complete your education, and fit you—unless some better fate intervene— for the position of governess or lady-teacher. What say you to that ? "

" May I ask who would defray the ex- pense ? "

" That is a small circumstance which hardly merits discussion."

" Pardon me, I think it of great con- sequence, my lord," replied Bell, with a proud flush.

"I would merely be repaying an obligation."

"Your lordship is, I fear, merely disguising your generosity."

He smiled, and made a deprecating movement with his hand.

"Let me interpret your feelings," he said, leaning back in his chair and gazing at her intently. "You think that by accepting this slight service you would be placing yourself in my dependence; that I would expect some return; that people might impute dubious motives to me or to you. Pray banish such ideas. You need never know of my existence — unless you choose. I would keep myself in the background, unless you preferred that I should be a principal figure in the tableau."

"I am confounded by your lordship's generosity," said Bell; "but perhaps, sir, you will explain your motive."

"Are you already so distrustful of human nature? Here am I with sufficient means, and with neither wife nor child. Why should I not feel a kindly impulse to assist a gentle, clever, and lovely girl ?—oh, I grant you that had Nature been less kind to you, I might have imitated her example. Who can tell? female merit is much commended by a pretty face. But, besides, your friends are all interested in your future. Miss Gordon, for example——"

Bell started, and looked inquiringly, almost distressfully, at him.

" Miss Gordon is a charming young lady, and I would do anything to pleasure her, but sentimental motives need not be imputed, if I may contradict an unspoken surmise. Then Mr Marjoribanks, and in a word every one of your friends, think something should be done; and as I have great influence with Mr Simpson, I am naturally expected to take the first step."

He was silent for a while, gazing at her downcast face, which betrayed her mental perplexity.

" No, my lord," she said at length ; " I am truly grateful, but I cannot accept your offer."

He seemed neither surprised nor disappointed.

"But if Mr Simpson himself sent you to a boarding-school, you would not object to go?"

"Most certainly I would object, my lord. I am of age to do something for myself. I know he would grudge the expense, and I will receive no benefit grudgingly bestowed."

"So proud? Well, 'tis only right and worthy of you. But my quiver is not empty yet. Has it ever struck you that possibly you are in no way related to Mr and Mrs Simpson?"

"I have long thought so, my lord, and the thought has been full of pain; for if so, I am an orphan, and my birth—ah, who can say what misery clings to it?"

Her eyes filled with tears, and he could see the tension of her clasped hands. He hesitated a few moments, rubbing his brow, and then said—

"'Tis evident, my dear child, that I am destined to be the reader of your fortunes, and here my function begins. Your birth is honourable, and you are a lady born."

When he had uttered the words, he drew

a deep breath and looked at her with a kind of tender suspense.

"*You* say so. Then it must be true. Thank God! thank God!" She covered her face with her hands to conceal the tears that came with a sudden outburst of blended emotion.

He went forward, and taking a chair beside her, gently laid his hand upon her head with a caressing touch. She shrank back a little and looked timidly at him, but the deep *humanity* of his gaze reassured her.

"Now, dear Isabel (for that is your name)," he said, in soft but thrilling tones, "you will expect the revelation of a mystery. Alas! 'tis as yet impossible. But the revelation is only postponed. Circumstances which I cannot disclose compel me to be silent till you come of age or till you marry. At either of these junctures you may appeal to me, and your appeal shall be answered."

"And I am only seventeen," murmured Bell, dejectedly.

"Time passes swiftly — all too swiftly, alas! 'Youth's a stuff will not endure,' as glorious Will says. Would that I could

' grow backward,' as he also says somewhere,
and meet you at some sweet intersection of
our paths.   But to come to business.   Your
birth being worthy of you, and your possession of means on coming of age being in-
herently probable—take my word for it, I
deceive you not—it follows that you may
freely accept any advance of funds from Mr
Simpson or from any one else without hesitation.   Well, what say you now ? "

"Are you my guardian, sir ? " she asked,
with a bashful and at the same time a wistful look.

"Your guardian ? " he repeated, huskily
and with evident emotion.   "Yes, your
guardian indeed !   Perhaps not in legal
strictness, but certainly in aim, intention,
and sufficiently accredited capacity.   Very
well.   All this being the case, it is manifestly necessary that you should acquire the
accomplishments which are the appanage of
a lady.   For you will ultimately, I hope,
take your place in society, and you must
be conversant with those graceful futilities
which mark caste.   You are in a sense well

educated, but you are not trained : you cannot dance a minuet, flirt a fan, or enamel
your conversation with French words and
phrases which very unjustly impute poverty
and inelegance to our mother-tongue. I confess I prefer your natural and unvarnished
refinement; but the decrees of fashion must
be respected. Every class of society has a
freemasonry of words, tones, gestures, which
only the initiated can use. Further, it is
the essence of fine manners to be unobtrusive
in everything; and even a charming and
idyllic rusticity is obtrusive. Society cannot endure angles — except in furniture.
Your fine young lady must cultivate a
graceful indifference of tone and sentiment;
her feelings must not speak above their
breath ; her real nature must be largely a
matter of conjecture; and the honeymoon
is a voyage of discovery to the adventurous
swain who wins this problematical being.
Forsooth, nobody would marry at all did
he not know that a young lady is also a
young woman with a heart and a head
waiting to be liberated. But I am too dis-

cursive. Nothing makes a man so eloquent as a sympathetic listener. And your lovely face is the mirror of my rhetoric. What say you now? Shall I draw another arrow from my quiver?"

"Indeed, my lord, I am so confused, amazed, bewildered by what you have told me, that I cannot reason. Is it all true? You would not, could not (oh, forgive the thought!) deceive a helpless girl."

"If I were capable of so foully wronging you," he replied, with passionate earnestness, "I would be the paltriest wretch that ever crawled and sneaked to an oblivious grave. You believe me, Isabel?" he asked, with a kind of imperious tenderness.

"I believe you, my lord," she replied, with a submissive and confiding look.

"Thank you. Now I am eager for a deeper intimacy with you, which I fear you will not grant me."

"I dare not, for many reasons, sir," said Bell, in a low tone. "Nor would you respect me if I did. And I aspire to your respect."

"Dear credulous girl!" he said, in vibrating tones, " the aspiration should be inverted. And yet I am not a villain. Who calls me villain ? "

He held his head to one side as if listening for some distant voice.

" Oh, do not say such words ! " she exclaimed in a pleading tone. " How could any one be so base and cruel as call you so ? "

" Kind, generous girl ! God—I bless you, if any blessing of mine—— But I am digressing again. What I wished to say was this : I desire a deeper intimacy, in all honour and sincere respect. But this may not be when I am ' Your lordship,' ' Sir,' and the rest of it. Away with these gilded additions ! Let me tell you a secret—not to be whispered till the proper hour arrives——"

" I do not like secrets, my lord. I pray you not to tell it," said Bell, with deep earnestness.

" 'Tis not a secret of which we have need to be ashamed. I would not inveigle you into duplicity or complicity. But secrecy is often synonymous with self-respect, not with duplicity. As Shakespeare says, 'The chariest maid is prodigal enough, when——' I forget the rest."

"But a secret between your lordship and me! Think of it, sir. I cannot express my thought as I would like, but you can divine it—you have so keen an intellect. How dangerous is an intimacy grounded upon a mutual secret! I have patience. Let me wait."

"So be it, you noble girl, worthy of your birth, worthy of the deepest respect, worthy of adoration. I shall say no more. And as regards what I *have* said, let me beg of you to conceal it, for weighty reasons. Have I your solemn promise?"

"If you desire it, most assuredly I shall. There is no shame in concealing brighter prospects."

"And as a compromise, try to think of me, try to call me, your guardian."

"I shall gladly so think of you, my lord."

"How formal!" he said, in a tone of reproach.

"Indeed, sir," she replied, with a blush

and a timid look, "I do not dislike to use the appellation."

His face brightened, and his lips moved as if he would fain speak, but the arrested utterance passed into a smile.

"Very well, my dear Isabel, very well. Now, our good friend downstairs will wonder at our protracted absence, unless he is deep in divinity or drink. To bring our conversation to a point : you will consent to my proposal ? "

"I shall be glad to enter a boarding-school —I know my deficiencies—but, I beg, not at your charges."

" Well, I dare not insist when your feeling is so strong. But if Simpson or his wife agrees——"

" I shall consent on condition that I recognise my obligation to repay them, if you assure me I shall be able so to do."

" And if they do not agree, then I shall see that money is raised upon your future prospects, — literally, I mean, and without any pious fraud—as if I were capable of anything pious ! "

"I beg of my guardian not to disparage himself," said Bell, with a bashful smile in which there was the faintest approach to archness.

"After that, what can I say?" he exclaimed, gently raising her hand to his lips. "Lo! I wear a halo. I am transfigured, translated. I strike the stars with my lofty head, as your friend Horace says. In all seriousness, I pray—I mean, may I acquire the power and the will, as I have the deep desire, to make my worth equal to your esteem. Now, my dear ward, let us go. What a memorable day for me!"

"And for me!" said Bell.

He took her hand to lead her from the apartment. Her cheeks were glowing, her head bent down; but it seemed as if her form had gained a new grace, a more elastic movement, a finer poise, which presented a vivid but harmonious contrast to the dignity and proud self-consciousness of his manhood.

They found Simpson peacefully slumbering in a comfortable arm-chair, and they exchanged a smile of amusement. He woke up, however, as they stepped into the room.

"I believe I hae been in the land o' nod," he said, rubbing his eyes. "Ye hae been a mortal lang while away, lassie. But women are a stiffnecked generation, and need a lecture as lang as the mainyard to get them to dae what a man would dae for a single word wi' a bit oath clapped ahint it. And noo, we maun be jogging hame."

CHAPTER IX.

SATAN'S HEAD.

THE fishing village of Fownie stands at the southern end of a long precipitous line of cliffs which fronts the German Ocean. Leaving the village and climbing the gradual acclivity which merges in this elevated ridge, you may walk for miles along the summit of the rocks, which here and there have been hollowed and honeycombed into caverns and blow - holes by the incessant action of the sea. About a mile and a half from the village is a semicircular bay, terminating at either end in two bluff promontories. The rocks consist of a solid base of sandstone surmounted by conglomerate, whereof the incrusted stones and pebbles, detached by the buffeting of the waves, have formed a shingly beach within the bosom of the bay.

Few sights are more beautiful than this pebbly stretch of shore, especially when it has been laved by the tide; for then it gleams with a rich variety of tints, pink and rose and yellow and amber, which diversify the predominating white. It is indeed a symphony of colour, whereof the white—not dull at such a time, but softly opalescent—is the basis. It is strange to think that this conglomerate, which was once a wave-washed shore, is again becoming a beach, and these pebbles, imprisoned for myriads of years, are returning to their ocean home once more. Compared with this vast cycle of change, the siege of Troy and the building of the Pyramids are as yesterday. But even this abacus of pebbles avails not to calculate the age of this fragment of the world; for what is pebble was rock slowly quarried by patient streams through long millenniums. "They are but dressings of a former sight."

Reflections such as these, though in a vaguer form, for geology was yet in embryo, passed through Andrew Prosser's mind as he wended his way along the cliffs. It was past mid-day, and a fog had descended upon the sea and shore. Wrapped in this shifting mass of vapour, the cliffs, bluffs, stacks of rock, pinnacles, and escarpments, seemed like the turbid phantasm of a dream. There was a heavy ground-swell, and the long billows tumbled in booming thunder into the caves, crannies, and tunnels with which the coast is indented. The long flat reefs, like natural moles and jetties, rose above the water, for the tide was only beginning to make; and the waves climbing above them fell back again in long cataracts down their perpendicular sides.

After half an hour's walk, Andrew reached that part of the coast opposite a huge isolated rock known by the weird name of Satan's Head. It emerged in massive grandeur from a rugged pavement of rock intersected by rough channels filled with the first influx of the tide. Its rudely hewn profile loomed out of the mist, solemn, defiant, implacable, and it required no great effort of the imagination to lend a kind of sinister life to the frowning features—the dark beetling brows, the aquiline nose, the inward notch of the mouth, the rugged chin; while two or three protuberances at the top of the colossal forehead simulated rudimentary horns. As Andrew advanced, the expression seemed to change when looked at from a different visual angle. The upper lip swelled into a portentous pout, the shade gathered more deeply into the sunken orbits. Andrew gazed long at this grotesque sculpture of the waves. He had often seen it before, but the mist gave a wider scope to shaping fancy. The anarchy of the sea had carved this congenial image of its wild havoc and ferocity. Even in fine weather it wears a look of mysterious malignity. It seems biding its time. The play of light and shade sets free a lurking grin, a mocking grimace. It tolerates the sunshine with contemptuous indifference, but is ever listening for the storm. It gives a purpose and coherence to the random wildness of these tormented cliffs. It concentrates and embodies the grim cruelty of nature.

Andrew continued his walk till he reached the shingly bay, and descending by a steep path, he toiled over the stones till he reached the entrance of a cave. As he advanced into its interior it grew darker, and at the farther end or recess formed by an elbow of the rocky passage there was total obscurity. The silence was broken by the tinkle and gurgle of a tiny spring which filtered out of the rock above and lost itself in the sandy bed of the cave, no doubt percolating downwards to the sea-level. Taking a small lantern from his pocket, Andrew struck a light, and, aided by the feeble glimmer, discovered a small niche or cranny in the rock. Inserting his hand, he drew out a small packet enveloped in oilskin. This he eagerly unrolled, and found the contents to be what he expected—a number of newspapers, political catechisms, broad-sheets, lampoons, pamphlets, and other varieties of the revolutionary literature of France. Some smuggling lugger had doubtless been the agency of transmission.

Sitting down on a ledge of rocks, he proceeded to examine his treasure by the dim light of his lantern. His appreciative enjoyment was, however, interrupted by the sound of approaching footsteps. He instantly extinguished his lantern, and hastily rolling up the papers into a rough parcel, put them back again into the niche from which he had removed them. Then he stood motionless and expectant. The newcomer appeared to have paused at the entrance of the cave. He was also evidently impatient, for he ground the pebbles beneath his heels, and occasionally smote his cane or walking-stick against the sides of the rocky cavity.

With infinite caution Andrew stole towards the salient angle of the passage and peered out. To his surprise he recognised Lord Wimpole. After a time that gentleman's impatience seemed to be diverted by a train of more agreeable reflections, for he began to hum with a true but somewhat dissonant voice some snatches of a French chanson, leaning the while against the wall of the cave.   Andrew listened, and could not help smiling as he caught the words, the dainty triviality of which seemed to suit so little the haughty, grim-visaged singer :—

> " Douce bergerette,
> Humecte tes pieds
> Des claires rosées ;
> L'aube se dessine
> D'une couleur si fine ;
> Quitte ta blanche couchette
> Douce bergerette
> Douillette ! "

> Douce bergerette,
> Cueillis le frais bouton
> Qui sent pour moi si bon,
> Parce qu'il contient
> Le parfum de ta main ;
> Ne te cache pas, finette,
> Douce bergerette,
> Douillette !

> L'aube, c'est ton sourire——"

The song was interrupted by the approach of another individual, who appeared to be in haste.   Lord Wimpole drew himself erect, and said in a tone of stern displeasure, "You have kept me waiting an unconscionable time, Simpson."

"I humbly beg pardon, my lord, but——"

"Explanations import a further loss of time," said Lord Wimpole, curtly. "Let us proceed to business. I suppose there is no risk of eavesdroppers here?"

"You may be sure there's naebody here," said Simpson, confidently. "Eh, but it's a damp, gruesome hole is this cave. I can understand why Abraham used the cave of Machpelah for a grave. I wadna come here after nightfall for a king's ransom. There's an uncanny sough aboot it. There hae been ghosts seen——"

"*Spirits* you mean," said Lord Wimpole, drily. "Now listen to me."

Andrew also prepared to listen. He had no squeamish scruples about eavesdropping in such circumstances. He scented roguery, and inwardly congratulated himself upon an opportunity which might not improbably be fruitful of important revelations. On the one hand his political prejudices suggested suspicion of an aristocrat, and on the other he had a very feeble faith in Simpson's honesty. Possibly, also, the study of French political literature led him to justify a proceeding repugnant to a British sense of honour. He therefore listened with both his ears.

"It is time, Simpson, that we made other arrangements regarding Miss Bell," began his lordship. "The maid grows wonderfully beautiful, and people are beginning to surmise that she is no relation of yours. Besides, the Anchor Inn is no place for her, nor are you the most fitting guardian for her."

"Maybe she is safer wi' me than she would be wi' your lordship," Simpson retorted somewhat sulkily. "I hae my principles, and if any impudent loon said an ill-guided word to Bell, I would keelhaul him properly. Naebody can say that I have neglected her. She has been well grounded in the Carritches, wi' the reasons annexed; and if that's no guid ballast for a lassie, I dinna ken what is."

" I am not blaming you. Your principles, though somewhat limited in their range, are sound enough so far as they go," said Lord Wimpole. " But she must now make a new departure. I propose that she should go to a boarding-school or ladies' seminary of some kind. We had a long conversation yesterday."

" The lassie was in a bit o' a fluther after it," said Simpson, suspiciously. " I'm no very sure that I acted richtly in taking her to see your lordship."

" What do you mean ? " demanded Lord Wimpole.

" Weel, ye see, you fine gentlemen, lords mair particularly, seem to think that, besides haein' the purple and fine linen and Benjamin's portion o' rich vivers, ye should also hae ony bonnie lassie that comes in your way. Now, to my thinking, the bonnie lassies should fall to the common lads, as a kind o' what Andrew Prosser calls a solatium for the lack o' the fine things *you* and those like you enjoy. It's no fair that you should hae everything. However, our time's coming. Whether would you like to be Dives or Lazarus a hundred years after this?" From the theological colour of this question, it may be surmised that Simpson had been " bowsing his jib."

" Well," replied Lord Wimpole, with a laugh, "I would like to be in some other person's bosom than Abraham's."

" Dinna be profane, my lord, if you please."

" I beg your pardon ; but we are irrelevant. As for our young friend's excitement, it was natural.   I told her she was not your niece."

" Hoots ! that's piper's news to her.   She has lang seen through that fable.   Ye must hae said mair than that."

" I said more than I have any intention of repeating," was the haughty rejoinder.

" I dinna want to ken what ye said ; but mind, I didna bring her up to be a fine gentleman's plaything."

" Forbear your insolence : her virtue is more precious to me than it can be to you."

" Ay, ay ! we a' mean to be good till temptation comes like a squall, and then we're on our beam-ends afore we ken where we are. I'll no hae her wranged. She's a winsome wee thing, for a' her pride."

"A winsome wee thing! Thank you for that, Simpson. You have well described her."

"Of course, if your lordship means to marry her, it's different. Ye might do waur. She's a bonny quean."

"A queen indeed! You are inspired to-day, Simpson. But this is not business. Tush! who can think of her and not deem everything else for the moment unworthy of a thought? She has bewitched me."

"It's a fine thing when our inclinations and our interests row in the same boat."

"What mean you by that?"

"Naething very particular. But it's sometimes difficult to make out which o' the twa things is rowing the stroke-oar."

"No innuendoes, if you please. What do you mean?"

"Weel, if I may be so bold, I think your lordship wants to get out of a difficulty by

marrying her. You might have adopted
her, if you meant kindly by her."

"I see I must make things clear to your
blundering intelligence. First, then, I almost hated her for long, as the daughter
of a favoured rival. She was the outward
token of my defeat. I was robbed of my
paternity. But that feeling has long van-
ished; it makes me shudder to think of it.
In the next place, I could not show any
manifest interest in her for a shoal of
reasons. People would have said she was
my child, the fruit of some obscure *amour*.
Then again, if my interest in her had been
too evident, she might imagine that she had
a claim on me, might expect me to be a fairy
godfather to her for the rest of her days,
might have become dissatisfied with her
station. On the other hand, she might be
too grateful, might become devoted to me
—'tis neck or nothing with romantic young
girls; they hate or they adore, as they
would describe their milk-and-water passions. Now, though I have not your noble
virtue, and have never learnt the Catechism

with the reasons annexed, I have never in
my most luxurious moods dreamt of doing
her harm. Her mother's memory has made
her sacred in my eyes, and will keep her
so. I hope you have followed this tedious
explanation. Well now, I have broken
ground. I have told her that she may
without loss of self-respect avail herself of
any means taken to better her education,
and I wish you to use your influence and
authority to determine her concurrence in
my plans."

"Weel, there is a lot to be said there-
anent. First and foremost, girls ding a' for
camsteariness. They ken their power. They
ken ye canna bang them aboot as ye would
a thrawn laddie. Why, they're madams
afore they're oot o' short frocks. Ye think
ye're getting on fine wi' a lassie, skimming
alang wi' a breeze abaft the beam, and you
at the helm priding yoursel' on your seamanship, when a' at ance she broaches to,
and ye maun let everything fly. Davy Jones
himsel' couldna steer them, the jauds! Then
there's another side to the question. If she

leaves me, I suppose your lordship means to withdraw aliment."

" Well, you would not expect to be paid for doing nothing. You have already feathered your nest well."

" Weel, ye see, I do expect to be paid for doing nothing, for what I might do might be inconvenient to your lordship."

" Oh, ho! blackmailing! Why, you shabby villain, I could ruin you. I could rack-rent you out of Fownie."

" Maybe ye could, I'll no say; and maybe you would like to do it. But it wouldna be safe. I dinna mean to be pitched overboard like Jonah. I dinna ask to sit in the cabin, but I expect a berth on board. Whales are no sae providential nowadays."

" Do you, in your wildest moments of im- pudence, hope to have *me* at your mercy?" demanded Lord Wimpole. " I am ready to defy any and every man, as I would defy the devil himself in his blackest pit."

" Whist! whist! ye God-forgotten sinner, that I should say so," cried Simpson, in hor- rified accents. " Ye are prood as Lucifer himsel' nae doot, and daring; I ken your heart is stout; but what becomes o' human pride and human daring, when the last trump sounds over land and sea? How will ye feel when ye hear your lang indictment read out? Ye will call on the rocks to hide you."

Lord Wimpole was for a few minutes silent. Simpson was not a pattern of virtue, but he was fervently orthodox, and his earnestness made him for the moment respectable.

"Every Scotchman is a theologian, as every Frenchman is an actor," resumed Lord Wimpole, sarcastically. "But to be practical. What knowledge do you possess which it would be worth my while to suppress? Out with it."

"I ken the exact date o' Bell's birth for ae thing. I ken other things forby. Na, na, Lord Wimpole, ye needna think to fling the glaiks in my een. I see through your plan. Ye want to marry the lassie so as to make yersel' safe. Your love, my lord, is a painted flame."

Andrew heard a furious oath, the sudden shuffling of feet, a half-choked exclamation of rage and terror, and peering out from his coign of vantage, he saw Lord Wimpole clutching Simpson by the throat, his features livid and distorted with the fierce emotions agitating him. Andrew sprang to his feet and ran towards the mouth of the cave.

"Hands off!" he shouted, and rushing up to Lord Wimpole, twined his hand within his silken cravat, and dragged him away from Simpson.

Lord Wimpole was for a moment confounded by Andrew's sudden apparition. In another instant he had grappled with him. Andrew was a man of exceptional physical power, but he had found his match, and it was only by the application of a wrestling trick that he was able to throw his antagonist. He fell heavily with him and upon him. Lord Wimpole lay quite still, while Andrew scrambled to his feet, and glanced anxiously round for some defensive weapon. Then Lord Wimpole sat up and

gazed silently at Andrew. His face was ashy
pale; his features, as it were, petrified in a
hideous mask of concentrated hate, while
beads of froth oozed out at the corners of
his lips. He rose slowly to his feet and
confronted Andrew.

"I shall settle scores with you afterwards," he said in a low voice.

"Aweel, my lord, you'll find my books
kept by Double Entry," said Andrew, stoutly,
"and you may be sure you'll get a receipt
in full."

"You insolent dog!" said Lord Wimpole,
grinding out the words through his clenched
teeth.

"You insolent aristocrat!" retorted Andrew, infusing into the epithet all its French
offensiveness.

Lord Wimpole cast one sinister look of
disdain and malignity at Andrew, and then,
with a careless glance at Simpson, strode
away from the cave. The two men listened
in silence to the churning and grating of
the shingle under his furious and precipitate
steps.

"Your bread's baked, my braw callant,"
muttered Simpson, with a white face and
trembling voice. "Ye had better take the
wings o' the morning and flee to the utter-
most parts o' the sea."

"Hoots awa'!" said Andrew, "I'm no
to be daunted wi' his catamountain looks.
Besides, you and I ken the chink in his
armour."

"Ye heard a' that was said?"

"Every doom's word. Now, Brother
Bonifacius, mind your oath!"

"This is no political matter, Andrew."

"You'll find it will turn out so. If that
tinselled knave seeks vengeance, it will be
through my political associations; and then
you'll hae to keep your weather-eye lifting
on your ain account."

Simpson grunted an unwilling assent, and
the two men set out homewards. The fog
had lifted, and the sun was shining brightly.
In the distance they could see Lord Wimpole's tall figure striding onwards like an
embodied Fate.

CHAPTER X.

LORD WIMPOLE STUDIES REVENGE.

THE two men walked along in silence till they reached the part of the cliffs fronting Satan's Head. Then Andrew said, "This is a fine quiet spot, Simpson. We'll sit down here, for you and I have an account to redd up."

A man who has just been half-throttled may be excused for being in a somewhat irritable state; and besides, Simpson was annoyed and dismayed that his conversation with Lord Wimpole had been overheard. Accordingly, he replied gruffly—

"Ye're aye catechising me, Andrew. But ye're no my father confessor, mind that. And besides, this is nane o' your business. Dinna scaud your fingers wi' other folk's kail. Ye'll find your ain het enough, if I'm no mista'en."

"Here's gratitude!" said Andrew. "But for me, your harns ran a chance of being plastered on the side of the cave."

"I'll no deny that ye did me a good turn; but, my certy, ye charge compound interest for any service ye dae me! What dae your copy-books say? 'Virtue is its ain reward.'"

"My copy-books also say, 'Honesty is the best policy.' Sit down, Simpson; you've got to hear me. I know enough to be dangerous, mind that."

Simpson seemed to feel the force of the remark, for he sulkily complied.

"Now, Simpson, I needna say that I didna intend to listen to your conversation. I was forced to listen, for I didna want to have to explain what I was doing in the cave. However, there's nae need for apologies. Everything is lawful against villany. When crime steeks the door, justice keeks in by the keyhole. And if justice is blind, as she is represented to be, the mair need for her to hae gleg hearing. Now, Simpson, you know all about Miss Bell, mair than even his braw lordship jalooses."

" That's my affair," said Simpson, doggedly.

" Is Brother Bonifacius a rogue ? " asked Andrew, cuttingly. " Does a Templar wrong an orphan ? "

" The Templars hae naething to do with this."

" Ay, but they have. We are republicans, and must cherish republican virtues. Do the Rights of Man not include the rights of orphans ? A man cannot be a pure patriot and a base traitor at the same time."

" Ye may talk, Andrew Prosser ; and i' faith, your tongue is like the clapper o' a mill ! It would deave the last trumpet——"

" Good ! " exclaimed Andrew with solemn exaltation. " You speak of the last trumpet. How will you stand then, with injustice done and villany concealed and connived at ? What says the grand Latin hymn—oh, the noble words !—

'Quidquid latet apparebit,
  Nil inultum remanebit,'

which means, that everything hidden will
come to light, and nothing shall remain un-
avenged. Think of that and tremble. If
you hide a wrong, you are an accomplice.
Even poor blindfolded Justice says that. An
orphan forby! There's much I dinna believe
in. The Calvinistic Deity is in my opinion
no more like the true Deity than—with rev-
erence be it spoken—the chalk caricatures
made of me by my saucy pupils resemble me ;
but, like the virtuous Robespierre, I believe
in the Supreme Being. And ye may be sure
that He has a mair tender feeling for orphans
than for any others of His creatures. He
must be in a deeper sense a Father to them,
to make up for the loss of an earthly father."

"Ye should hae been a minister, Andrew,"
said Simpson, considerably impressed by this
long harangue, and recovering his ingratiating manner.

"Man, Simpson, ye hae nae mair sense
than a canary, which whistles loudest at
family worship," said Andrew, with impatient
disgust. "What is the connection between
Bell and that titled villain?"

" Ye heard for yoursel'."

" True enough, I didna put my ears in my pocket ; but hearing is one thing and understanding another."

" Ye must be satisfied wi' this, that I'll no see Bell wranged. I'll bide my time till everything is ready, and then——"

" How many years' purchase of your life hae ye got, Simpson ?" asked Andrew, solemnly.

" If I die, there's documents," was the reply.

" Where are they ? "

" In a safe place."

" I see how it is. Ye hae got a dumb spirit in you. But I have not."

" Ye never said a truer word than that," rejoined Simpson with a gruff laugh.

" I'll bring the matter up at the first Chapter of the Templars, and then you'll be forced to give an account of yourself."

" Here's fine liberty o' the subject, if a body has to tell his private affairs. Afore ye put down the tyranny o' Governments, put down your ain tyranny."

"Bide a wee, Brother Bonifacius. Obedience is the first duty of man; the only question is, what and whom he has to obey. Is it to be a senseless despotism, or an enlightened and beneficent authority?"

"Knight Templars here or Knight Templars there, I'll keep my affairs to mysel'," said Simpson, obstinately.

"Is that your last word?"

"That's the end o' the chapter," said Simpson with a grin.

"Then I wash my hands of the consequences. Mind, I'll no rest. Dearly as I love liberty, I love justice mair. You are a marked man, Simpson."

"Threats?"

"Yes," said Andrew, with a heightened colour. "The Templars represent the true type of society in which a man shall be compelled to do right, or become a fugitive and a vagabond like Cain."

"Ye needna craw sae crouse, Andrew Prosser," replied Simpson, with a dark scowl. "If you dae me an ill turn, you'll rue it. There's twa can play at clypin'."

"My braw man, if you turn informer you had better order a suit of armour, an iron mask, and a brazen tower to live in, for I wouldna gie a plack for your life. Get you gone, miserable wretch!"

Simpson growled some unintelligible words, and with a parting look of fear and hatred, set off at a good round pace for Fownie; while Andrew retraced his steps to the cave to recover his packet of papers.

Simpson, however, had not gone far before he suddenly came upon Lord Wimpole at a turn of the path. He was standing motionless, with his arms crossed upon his broad chest, and with his cane forking out behind him, as if in readiness for an instant blow. Perhaps he had expected to encounter Andrew. The heavy scowl upon his brow relaxed when he caught sight of Simpson, and he unclasped his arms.

"I am of few words, Simpson," he said, with a lordly look in little consistency with the apology which he now offered. "I have done you an outrage. Accept either my apology or a sum of money as solatium."

"I am satisfied wi' the apology," replied Simpson in a surly tone; "but I would advise you next time to keep your ten commandments aff a body's thrapple."

"Enough said! You have accepted my apology, and I love not to drink the lees of a quarrel. Moreover, the indignity has been as much mine as yours. I wish you to come in the course of an hour to Swinton Hall. We have need of further consultation."

"Aweel, if you promise no to mishandle me——" Simpson began.

Lord Wimpole's eyes flashed, and bending forward so as to gaze into Simpson's eyes, at the same time stretching forward his long and powerful forefinger, and pointing it at Simpson's throat, he said in a low tone—

"I shall never strike you again, Simpson; it will depend upon yourself whether I kill you or not. Now, will you come?"

"Ay, I'll come," Simpson replied, with an abject look of fear.

Accordingly, after Simpson had returned to the Anchor Inn, had composed his agi-

tated nerves with a stiff dram, and had re-
paired the disorder of his attire, he set out
for Swinton Hall.

He was ushered into the library as on the
previous occasion, and found Lord Wimpole
tranquilly seated at his escritoire.

"Take a seat, and excuse me for a brief
instant," said that gentleman, in a more
gracious tone than was habitual with him.
"Meanwhile, help yourself to a glass of wine
or spirits. I take very little of these things
myself, because I don't desire to go to the
devil before my time."

Simpson, nothing loath, complied with the
invitation, and Lord Wimpole finished his
letter. Having done so, he rang the bell,
and directed that the missive should be
instantly conveyed to Mr Gordon, senior.
Then he sat down, leaned back in his chair,
threw one leg over the other in an easy
posture, and confronted Simpson with a
smile of demure mockery.

"Talking of the devil, Simpson, I have
sometimes thought that he is a distillation,"
he began.

"A—distillation?" repeated Simpson, with his glass half-way to his lips.

"Ay, you are a theologian, and have no doubt some light—lurid light—on the subject."

"The less said aboot him the better," replied Simpson. "He's a chiel that has got lang ears."

"Ay, the devil is an ass, no doubt; for why should he persist in doing evil when he knows he will be defeated in the long-run? And since his business is a losing one, why should we not all leave his sooty forge, where we help to make his fiery darts? Or to change the metaphor, why should we not cease to run his contraband spirits, and pay duty to the King, as we should? Come, shall we give up the illicit traffic, and try honesty for a change?"

"If you think you can afford to do it," said Simpson, slowly.

"That I can, and that I would have you know," said Lord Wimpole, emphatically. "I believe I have finished my apprenticeship; or if not, I can always run my indentures."

"You are speaking in parables, my lord; and as I am a plain man——"

"Oh, you are shrewd enough, Simpson, shrewd enough. And being orthodox, you will take care not to give the devil too strong a purchase. But if you thought he were only a distillation, what then?"

"Ay, what then?" echoed Simpson, with a bewildered stare.

"You will not pare an inch off his claws, or abridge his tail, such is your orthodoxy. And yet, he is merely a distillation. Your heart and mine, Simpson, is the still, and wicked thoughts are the vapours which, when condensed, form this potent spirit. Now perfumes, delicious perfumes, giving sweetness to beauty in itself far more sweet, may also be distilled. What say you if we distil perfumes instead of this rank and fiery spirit?"

"Weel, my lord, you hae doubtless a meaning, but I wish you would distil it," said Simpson, with a laugh.

"I shall do so," said Lord Wimpole, with an abrupt transition to sternness. "You think I have a guilty secret, and you think to trade upon it. You expect hush-money; you hope to keep me in a shivering, slinking, base submission. You do not know your man, Simpson. If there is a single deed of mine hid in the shadows of my past life which should threaten my ruin, then I should appeal to goodness, not to cupidity. You are warned. I truckle to no one for any poor boon my life affords. You understand me now?"

"Yes, I understand you, my lord," replied Simpson, "and I never had any intention o' fashing your lordship; but that's nae reason why another man should share our secrets."

"You mean Prosser, I suppose?"

"Yes. He kens ower muckle or suspects ower muckle."

"I understand he is a friend of yours."

"Andrew would tire out the best friend he ever had. He is dominie out o' school as weel as in it. A dog daurna wag his tail in Fownie without Andrew's leave. He has a grievous tongue, has Andrew. I think a change o' air would dae him good."

" I agree with you : he is a pragmatical, prying scoundrel."

" That's ower strang a word. He means weel."

" To the Government ? "

" As for that, I'll sae naething. I'll no sow hemp-seed for my ain neck."

" They say he is a member of a secret society : is that true ? "

" There's a lot o' clishmaclavers in a wee place like Fownie. Folks will be suspecting me next."

" Very probably. How came he to be in the cave to-day ? "

" This is the Wednesday half-holiday, and he would be taking a daunder alang the shore. And that reminds me, he'll be gangin' to Dundee in the evening."

" For what purpose ? "

" To see his Aunt Jane."

" Or some other Jane."

" Na, na ; Andrew's a respectable lad. I'll no hae his character abused. His auntie is a widow woman, and needs help in making up her books and writing out orders. I hae

seen her mysel', so that's proof positive ; and
she's a douce canny body, though she's aye
craikin' aboot her ailments. Of course, he
may hae other business to transact. We
hae nae richt to take precognition o' his
doings."

"Then he probably goes on some political
errand. Don't you think so ? "

"I neither meddle nor make wi' politics.
For what says the Preacher ? 'Curse not the
king, no not in thy thought ; for a bird of
the air shall carry the voice, and that which
hath wings shall tell the matter.' He was a
wise man, was Solomon, except that he had
ower mony wives. I find ane enough, and
whiles mair than enough."

Lord Wimpole leant lazily forward and
picked up a paper-cutter, with which he
amused himself by making passes through
the air as if he were lopping off the heads
of poppies.

"Your principles do you honour, Simpson,
in a general way, but veracity is not one
of them. Alas ! many an inventor of fiction
is lost to literature for want of a good edu-

cation.   And conversely, may we not say
that creative art acts sometimes like a seton
or cataplasm, and draws away the peccant
humours?   But I am wasting time.   Not-
withstanding your profession of political
indifference, Simpson, you are yourself a
member of a Secret Society ; and if I wished
to suppress you, how easy it would be!"

Simpson started to his feet with blanched
cheeks and glaring eyes.

"My lord, you are jesting," he faltered.
"You—you——"

"Sit down, my good man.   I can keep a
secret as well as you.   I intend you no
harm.   But you will answer me a few questions, if you please.   When does Prosser go
to Dundee?"

"About six o'clock.   But——"

"Give me leave.   I think there is time.
I can get a warrant of arrest, and set the
town-officer of St Thomas to work by that
time."

"But, my lord——"

"Give me leave.   He takes the usual
coach-road?"

"Yes.   But surely, my lord——"

"Pray do not interrupt.   You are safe enough.   Will he be armed?"

"He'll hae a stout walking-stick, and he'll use it, my lord.   Wow, but Andrew will fecht!   You had better gie the idea up. It's an unchancy affair."

"Well, I could get John Wilkie to help," said Lord Wimpole, thoughtfully.   "John hates Republicans, as the devil hates holy water."

"John Wilkie! his wooden leg is a sair impediment.   Of course he has his cutlash. But it wouldna be wise to use it.   Andrew will be like a lion in the swellings of Jordan, and that's a sma' comparison."

"So much the worse for Prosser.   It will be deforcement."

"He'll no mind what they call it.   He'll fecht like Apollyon in the Valley of Humiliation.   Na, na, my lord; wait till ye get a squad o' soldiers, if ye must hae your revenge on the puir fellow.   Eh, but I'm wae for him!"

"You wish to gain time for warning him.

I tell you there is no intention of proceeding
against your Associated Order, or whatever
you call it.   We merely wish to lop off an
excrescence.   Doubtless you would require to
be circumspect, but a long career of smuggling has made you a master of craft and
subterfuge."

"But what has led your lordship to think
that I would be sic a daft gowk, sic a red-
wud, senseless, glaikit idiot"—he went on,
gnashing his teeth—"as to join ony un-
lawfu', seditious, treasonable society ?   I wad
hae nae mair brains than a tomtit——"

"Yes ; that reminds me that one of your
confederates is a bird-fancier," said Lord
Wimpole, with a mischievous smile.

"Oh Lord !   Guid be gracious to us !
Here's a bonny kettle o' fish !   But if the
warst comes to the warst, I'll make a clean
breast o' it.   I'll no be hanged and quartered
for a lot o' ranting, raving, bletherin' loons.
Oh Lord ! what will my wife say ? "

He sat down in his chair, trembling in
every limb, while Lord Wimpole surveyed
him with a mocking smile.

"Pooh, pooh! Simpson, you take too tragic a view of the matter," he said, after a considerable interval, during which Simpson's imagination had ample time to erect a gibbet. "I pledge you my protection. Be under no alarm. You will not be incriminated or molested. Now I must be off. Pray excuse me if I terminate this interview somewhat abruptly. There is just one thing I must beg. Don't warn Prosser —it might be dangerous. And now, good day to you. Help yourself to a glass of spirits. You are somewhat perturbed."

So saying, he nodded blandly, and left the room.

CHAPTER XI.

BLESSED ARE THE PEACEMAKERS.

SIMPSON wended his way homewards in a
daze, with but one thought luridly bright
in the hazy horror of his mind—the thought,
namely, that he was a ruined man. For
if Andrew were arrested, as seemed likely,
and compromising documents were found in
his possession revealing the existence, the
haunt, and the membership of the Knight-
Templars, his own connection with that
treasonable society was certain to come to
light. Lord Wimpole had endeavoured to
reassure him ; but was it not manifestly his
lordship's interest to get rid of him? At
times, in the whirl and turmoil of his
thoughts, the recollection of the grimly

smiling nobleman whisking off the heads
of imaginary flowers pictured itself before
his imagination, and he shuddered. The
whole interview indeed, though his mind
was too turbid to reproduce its details, had
left an abiding sense of Lord Wimpole's
formidable superiority of intellect, will, and
daring; and he fervently resolved that if,
by a happy chance, he escaped the present
imminent danger, he would never again
provoke a conflict with so terrible an
antagonist.

But in the meantime, what was he to do?
Despite Lord Wimpole's warning, he resolved to give Andrew an intimation of
danger.

While he had been at Swinton Hall, Bell
had been seated in the little private parlour
of the inn making a head-dress — bonnets
were not then in vogue—for Mrs Simpson.
The basis of this structure was a headpiece of jonquille-coloured silk artistically
crumpled, from the summit of which soared
three diverging feathers forming the " pan-
ache," as it was called.

As Mrs Simpson was tall and stout, Bell could not think of the appearance which the portly dame would present without a mingled feeling of awe and dismay.

Mrs Simpson, meanwhile, standing with her arms akimbo, watched the young girl's manipulations with admiring interest and anticipative delight.   Her face was large and powerful, the massive features being nobly moulded, and she had a magnificent head of coal-black hair, so that Bell often thought she might have served as a model for a Roman empress.

A kind and generous heart beat within that exuberant bosom ; but alas ! she was at times unable to resist the blandishments of her husband's cognac. When she indulged this weakness, her whole nature appeared to be transformed.   At the slightest provocation she fell into a paroxysm of blind and irresponsible fury, in which her great strength made her supremely dangerous. At such times her husband deemed it prudent to lurk in cautious seclusion ; and even Bell, who with all her gentleness was high-spirited, shrank from the unfortunate woman with nervous trepidation.

For once, but only once, Mrs Simpson had struck her so violent a blow as to render her unconscious. The unhappy woman was sobered at once by the act, and her contrition had been as violent in its expression as the rage which had preceded it. She tore her hair, and beat her bosom ; and when Bell had come to herself, overwhelmed the girl with passionate caresses and floods of repentant tears. The blow had never been repeated, and Bell was henceforth the only one who could in some measure moderate the transports of her intoxicated frenzy. When she felt the terrible craving assert its tyranny, for her fits of intoxication seemed a kind of physical crisis, she would implore Bell to watch her, and keep her out of temptation as far as possible.

As Bell grew up, she became increasingly successful in warding off these excesses, which seemed rather a kind of demoniacal possession than a voluntary self-indulgence. Though the word dipsomania had not yet been in-

vented, and cleptomania was more succinctly
denominated thievery, there can be little
doubt that Mrs Simpson was the victim of
an inherited propensity for drink.

She was an Englishwoman, whom Simpson
had met and married at Portsmouth. His
feelings towards his wife were somewhat
complicated. He was proud of her, but in
his inmost heart profoundly afraid of her,
for he was conscious that her most favour-
able attitude towards him was one of good-
natured tolerance not unmingled with contempt. Under the influence of cognac she
became at once aggressive. She was fas-
tidiously clean and tidy in her habits, and
Simpson's neglect of the minor graces of
dress and deportment affected her with a
feeling of almost physical repulsion. She
had the reputation of being "near" in
money matters, of which she had the sole
management, though Simpson cheated her
with comically transparent artfulness, and
secreted little hoards with a kind of magpie
subtlety. She had, however, a good excuse
for her parsimony ; she was bent on accumu-

lating a "tocher" for Bell. She had never
had a child of her own, and all her baffled
maternity spent its affection on her "little
lass."

"You are quick with your fingers, dear,"
remarked Mrs Simpson, after a long silence.
"You would make a good milliner."

"I sometimes thought of learning that
occupation," Bell replied, "when I have been
in perplexity about my future."

Mrs Simpson shook her head.

"Better things are in store for you than
that," she said, in a somewhat melancholy
tone. "You will leave me, I fear, ere long,
and then what will become of me without
you, my dear?"

"We won't speak of that, dear aunt," said
Bell, affectionately.

"We shall have to speak of it; I know
what is being said. Everybody knows that
you should not be in a common inn, but
should be getting the education proper for
a young lady. And so you should, no doubt.
But you won't look down on your poor aunt,
will you? I have never wronged you. I

know nothing of your birth or parentage, my dear; and if you had been my own daughter, I could not have loved you more."

"I know that, dear. I have never felt the misery and sad dependence of an orphan, thanks to your fond affection."

"It is good of you to say so. But things are shaping, I know well. Lord Wimpole and my man have been a good deal together of late, and something is brewing. But his lordship shall not make a cat's-paw of the silly oaf."

"I am sure Lord Wimpole means me no harm."

"Little you know, you sweet innocent! He is a fine and stately man, no doubt, and perhaps too proud for ordinary vices, but there's a canker at his heart. He is like one of the grand old oaks which I have seen in my native county of Hereford, fair to see, but all decayed within. Wait till a storm comes."

"I doubt you are prejudiced, dear aunt," said Bell, in a low voice.

"It is natural for you to think so, darling, knowing little of the evil of this deceitful world. When I was your age," she went on, with a sigh and a downcast look, "I thought the same. I was a lady's-maid in my young days. If I could forget all that happened then, maybe I would not need the devil's comfort that I crave for, God forgive me! Put away that silly gewgaw, my dear," she added, pointing to the headdress; "it sickens me to see it. Women, young and old, are empty fools, who would peril their soul's salvation for a painted rag or a glittering stone. Strange that worms should spin a covering for what the worms must so soon consume. Away with it, my dear! But when I said all women were fools, I didn't mean you, God bless you!"

She strained the young girl to her bosom, tenderly kissed her, and then went up-stairs.

Shortly after, Simpson entered the parlour.

"What is the matter, Mr Simpson?" asked Bell, alarmed by his disordered looks and almost convulsive movements.

He threw himself into a chair with a heavy groan, and wiped away the cold sweat that bedewed his brow.

" What's the matter, quo' she ! " he replied, irritably.   " Everything's the matter."

Then with a sudden change to self-commiseration, " Eh, lassie, lassie ! " he groaned out, " ' Strong bulls of Bashan have compassed me about ; ' or at least there's ane that has tossed me and gored me, and means, I think, to trample the life out o' my miserable body.   ' Put not thy trust in princes,' Bell, nor in lords — the lords o' justiciary least of all, God be mercifu' to me ! "

" Shall I go for my aunt ? " asked Bell, who was beginning to be seriously alarmed.

" What ! go for my aunt — I mean my wife—ye daft limmer ? " repeated Simpson, in great dismay.   " Na, na ; she would be Job's wife to me this day.   Where is she ? "

" Up-stairs."

" That's ae drop o' comfort in my bitter cup.   Now, steek the door, my dawtie.   I dinna want Peggy to hear what I hae to say.

And if ye dinna understand, for God's sake dinna deave me wi' questions, for my head is bummin' like a bees' byke.   Now listen to me, Bell.   Ye maun ken that Andrew Prosser and Lord Wimpole hae had a bit tuilzie, and his lordship is neither to haud nor to bind ower it."

"Oh, I am grieved to hear it," said Bell; "but why——"

"There ye begin, ye silly tawpie," said Simpson, peevishly.   "Can ye no stop your gab for twa minutes?   I was saying they had a scuffle thegither, and his lordship is hot for revenge——"

"Oh, do not say that!" protested Bell; "he is too high-minded——"

"There ye gang again!" cried Simpson, clapping his hands to his head; "what wi' dominies, lords, and lassies, life in this God-forgotten place is nae better than the valley of Jehoshaphat.   *Will* ye listen, ye gibbie-gash?"

"Not if you speak to me in that way, Mr Simpson," said Bell, proudly.

"Eh, but ye're a thrawn huzzie, Bell!

Ye needna take the dorts, lassie; as I am this day, my words are like the sparks that fly upwards. Ye're a kind-hearted creature, I ken that brawly."

" Well, I shall try not to interrupt," said Bell.

" Thank goodness for that ! Weel, ye see, Lord Wimpole is thinking o' getting Andrew arrested. Hooly now, Bell! Whether a man can be arrested for a common assault or no, I dinna ken; the lawyers, confound them, ken that best. But the affair is mair fankled than that. That's but a drop in the bucket. For, ye see, Andrew and me are members o' a kind o' club or society—freemasons like — and the Government is suspicious o' a' societies at this time. Forby that, there's a sough abroad that Andrew is disloyal, and maybe this is a roondaboot way o' getting him into the cleiks o' the law. So I want you to warn him. He'll be gangin' to Dundee the nicht — tell him he's no to gang on nae account whatever. He maun juik and let the jaw gae by. Do ye understand that, my dawtie ? "

"Tolerably well; but oh, Mr Simpson, things are far worse than you have hinted."

Simpson groaned.

"I misdoot ye're no far wrang, lassie. But do as I tell ye. Ye'll gang to Andrew, and ye'll say to him first, 'When is lint in the bell?'—though, my certy, hemp would be the properer word, wae's me! After that ye'll say, 'An Achan is in the camp.' These are passwords, ye ken, and will let him see that ye hae your credentials, so to speak. Do ye understand that, my dear."

Bell nodded.

"Then ye'll warn him no to leave Fownie this nicht, nor for mony a nicht to come."

"But why do you not warn him yourself?" asked Bell.

"Why do I not warn him mysel', quo' she?" said Simpson, evidently staggered by the question. "Weel, ye see, Andrew and I hae had words. He would slam the door in my face, that would he. Or if he did listen to me, he would gang against my advice to spite me. That cock winna fecht, lassie. But he'll be guided by you; you can row folks rcond your little finger. So rin awa', my dawtie, and do your errand, and I'll be muckle obleeged to you."

"Very well; I'll do my best, Mr Simpson," said Bell.

Simpson appeared to be much relieved.

"Naebody can say now that I didna act the part o' the good Samaritan," he said, self-complacently. "Only, folks shouldna gang to Jericho if they can help it. Eh, but I'll remember this on my last bed, and it will be a comfort to me. My auld mither—rest her soul!—would hae been prood o' me this day."

So saying, he left the parlour, and Bell heard him presently clinking glasses behind the bar.

As Bell went up the village street towards the schoolhouse, the goodwives of the place, who all thought her an "upsetting quean," leaned on their domestic brooms or wiped the soap-suds from their brawny arms to exchange appropriate comments.

"There's the little madam," said one, in a pregnant whisper.

"She's in an unco fluther," remarked a neighbour gossip.

"She's fell prood," said another.

"She's aye been finger-fed, ye see. She's the English wife's dawtie. I'm thinkin' she was a' the tocher Sam got wi' his braw wife."

"Fat for suld that stunkered-looking loon be hand in glove wi' Tam? Ay, ay, the cat aye kens the road to the kirn."

"She's no sic a burning beauty when a' is said," remarked a stout dame, sourly. "She's but a shilpit willow-wand o' a lassock. The deil confound her dirty pride!"

"Hoots, Mrs Flucker, the lassie's weel eneugh!" protested another gossip. "She canna help being genty. She's got guid bluid in her. Some lord's bye-blow, nae doot."

"What's bred in the bane will come oot in the flesh. She's gangin' her mither's gait, I trow."

"The nicht afore last," said another, in a mysterious whisper, "his lordship stood for a lang while staring at her window. It had chappit ten, and I was looking oot for my man : I saw him wi' my ain een."

Meanwhile Bell, anxiously preoccupied, and unconscious that she was running the gauntlet of censorious criticism and speculation, had sped her way to the schoolhouse. Mrs Badger was evidently astonished to see her, and on being asked whether Andrew was in, replied—

"Ay, he's in ; but let me tell ye, Bell Simpson, it's no seemly for a young lassie to come speerin' after an unmarried man."

"Oh, Mrs Badger !" exclaimed Bell, with a burning blush. "I am sent by Mr Simpson to see Andrew on serious business," she faltered, and then burst into tears.

"Come in," said Mrs Badger more gently. "He's in his room dressin'. He is gangin' to see his Aunt Jane, ye ken." And she pursed her lips.

"Pray tell him I am anxious to see him," faltered Bell, struggling with her emotion.

"Dinna greet, lassie," said Mrs Badger. "It was only a word o' warnin'. We are a' frail creatures. Dinna greet. Ye'll hae plenty o' time to dae that afore ye're as auld as me. If a' the tears I hae shed were put into a bottle, as the Psalmist says, it would need to be a big ane. I'll chap at his door."

In a few minutes Andrew appeared.

"Ah, Miss Bell!" he exclaimed, with a beaming smile, "I'm blithe to see you. But you seem disturbed."

"Mr Prosser, I was told to say to you, 'When is lint in the bell?'"

Andrew started and looked intently at the young girl. Then his face flushed, and his eyes sparkled angrily.

"Anything else, Miss Bell?"

"He bade me also say, 'Brother, there is an Achan in the camp.'"

"And what right has that shabby scoundrel to inveigle a young maid into a compromising situation? Ay, ay, he's all of a piece; there's neither honesty nor honour in his fause heart. And he is the Achan, no other; and I well know the reason. Anything else, Miss Bell?"

"He warns you not to go to Dundee this

evening. From his manner, I feel sure that he knows of danger threatening you."

"Danger of arrest?"

"I fear so. Oh, Mr Prosser, be persuaded and do not go!"

"Not go? I would go if the road were paved with red-hot coulters—or at least I would try. Am I the man to prate about liberty, and then creep into a mouse-hole when my personal liberty is threatened? Besides, this is most probably a ruse on his part."

"Really I do not think so," said Bell. "Mr Simpson seemed terribly agitated and alarmed."

"That's good news, and he'll be mair agitated and alarmed when I meet him."

"Andrew, be sensible for aince," said Mrs Badger, earnestly, "and dinna gang to Dundee. There's nae call for ye to thrust your hand into the cockatrice's den."

"Ay, but there is, Mrs Badger—that I may grip it and squeeze the venomous reptile to death. And in short," he continued in a melancholy tone, "I care little what befalls me. I have lost what is far more precious than liberty. Let the tow gang wi' the bucket."

"Oh, do not say so!" said Bell, tearfully. "Your friends would be truly grieved if any misfortune happened to you."

"Ah, Miss Bell, replied Andrew, with a sad smile,

> ' Most friendship is feigning,
> Most loving—mere folly!'

That it is, mere folly, though at the time it may seem heavenly sweet. And as for friends, how many friends had Job when his calamities came thick and fast? His wife told him to curse God and die—no doubt she wanted another man. Then his friends : did they help him to build his house, or club together to buy a wheen cows and sheep for him? No they. He scarted himself with potsherds, and they scarted him with censorious speeches;" and Andrew glanced at Mrs Badger, who was sitting fidgeting with her apron.

"Verily this is a valley of Baca," she whimpered, hastily brushing away a few tears from her eyes. "Oh, Andrew, dinna be thrawn. Bide at hame the nicht."

"Never!" cried Andrew, hotly. "I'm low enough, God knows; poor enough in purse and reputation; and—and—yes, I am low enough, but I would indeed be still lower, at the very bottom of the abyss of ignominy, if I ceased to respect myself, and having denounced the Pharaoh who oppresses the People, trembled at the rumble of his chariots. I'll face this danger, whatever it is."

"A wilfu' man will hae his way," said Mrs Badger, with a heavy sigh. "But let me tell you, my puir Andrew, ye should take mair thocht o' your life, considering how little prepared ye are for the losing of it, as I sadly fear."

"Our Maker isna as anxious as an earthly monarch to find His creatures guilty of treason. He will quash many an indictment, I firmly believe."

"Mrs Badger, will you oblige me with writing-paper?" asked Bell, gently.

"That I will, my hinnie," said Mrs Badger,

gulping down a sob; "for, so far as puir human nature can be guid, you are guid, as I weel believe. A kind-hearted lassie ye are, and a bonnie; and eh, if ye had but the robe of imputed righteousness, ye would be indeed a daughter o' the King o' Zion, all glorious within and without!"

She went into Andrew's parlour and presently returned with writing materials. Then she sat down on a stool before the fire, and now and then furtively wiped away a tear. Andrew, meanwhile, leaning against the wall, gazed affectionately at the young maiden, as, seated at the kitchen table, she wrote the following lines :—

"My Lord,—Having learned to my great distress that you and Mr Prosser have had an altercation, and that you are bitter against him (with what degree of justice I know not), insomuch that you design to proceed to extremities with him, which, I fear, import his utter ruin, I venture to take the great liberty (for which I hope your lordship will pardon me) of interceding on his behalf.   He does not and shall not know of this proceeding on my part, and would perchance resent it; but I owe him much gratitude for all his kindness to me, and he is, when understood, a very worthy and honourable man.   I would therefore submissively entreat your lordship to show as much lenity and indulgence in this matter as you can.   I add no more, for if my entreaties do not avail, much less will my arguments.— I rest, your lordship's most obedient servant,

"ISABEL SIMPSON."

Having folded up and wafered this missive, she prepared to go.

"I suppose I must not ask, Miss Bell, to whom you have addressed this letter?" said Andrew.

"That must remain a secret, Mr Prosser," said Bell, colouring.

Andrew bowed and smiled; and then Bell, having shaken hands with Mrs Badger, took her leave.

"Isn't she a dear sweet creature that?" said Andrew.

"Her lips drop honey and the honeycomb,"
replied Mrs Badger, tremulously. "Oh, what
a wearifu' warld! what a wearifu' warld!
Everything's wrang! When, oh! when, will
He come, whose right it is to reign?"

Andrew noiselessly returned to his parlour.

Bell now stepped out briskly for Swinton
Hall. At the sight of each traveller in the
distance her heart was contracted with a
spasm of terror, for she feared that he might
be Lord Wimpole. She reached the Hall,
however, without encountering him, and
having delivered the letter at the door to
the elderly female who had admitted her on
the occasion of her previous visit when accompanied by Simpson, she turned quickly
away from the house and re - entered the
avenue. But those whom we do not wish
to see have an uncomfortable trick of making
their appearance; and she had not advanced
more than a few yards when she caught sight
of Lord Wimpole at the farther extremity of
the leafy vista.

Her heart gave so violent a throb that she

thought she would have fainted, her knees
trembled beneath her, and her feet felt like
lead as she advanced slowly to meet him,
struggling the while to gain some degree of
self-command.   He was mounted, and his
horse was flecked with foam, as if it had
been hard driven.   No sooner did he espy
her than he sprang to the ground, and
greeted her with ceremonious politeness,
though there was a bright and elated look
in his dark eyes.

" I have left a note for your lordship, which
will explain my errand," she said, pantingly.

" Letters, my dear Isabel, are but halting
substitutes for speech.   Pray tell me your
errand."

" I have made a request."

" 'Tis granted, to the utmost circumference
of my poor ability."

" Oh, sir, I thank you !" said Bell.   " The
matter is this : we fear that you mean to
punish Mr Prosser for his temerity in assail-
ing you."

He frowned, and fixed his penetrating gaze
upon the young girl.

"Will nothing cure that clown's blabbing indiscretion?" he exclaimed, with vicious energy. Then more lightly: "I beg pardon. Methinks, dear child, the branks were more suited for men than for women. But permit me to correct a misunderstanding. Prosser, no doubt, is a fussy presumptuous fellow; and he certainly laid hands on me, as I on him. It is impossible to say who was really the aggressor: we rushed at one another with the impetuosity, though not with the tenderness, of a lover and his lass; and when both are equally willing, it is dividing a hair 'twixt upper and nether side to demand who kissed first. But I wound your delicacy. Enough. I bear him no grudge. He is a man of courage, and I respect such. But alas! my dear Isabel, his political principles are deplorable, I have not been able to overlook the reports current as to his disaffection, and it appeared to me that the time had come to institute searching inquiries."

"Ah, sir, you have destroyed my last hopes!" said Bell, sadly.

"Had I known you would have taken the

matter so to heart, I would have left to
others the duty of investigating the amount
of truth in these rumours regarding him.
As for the assault, pray think no more of
it.   He shall not be molested on that account.   And as for his possible arrest and
examination, I shall endeavour to prevent
it, or at least avert serious consequences.
Rest assured I shall do my utmost for him
—my utmost.   My credit, protection, and
purse are at his disposal."

"Ah, my lord, this is indeed generous!"
said Bell, gratefully.

"I am amply rewarded by your good
opinion.   And I shall set off presently on
your mission of mercy.   But what did Mr
Simpson say?"

"Indeed, my lord, he was so confused and
agitated that I had some difficulty in understanding him."

"How few people can keep a secret,
Isabel!   But you can, I trow."

"When necessary, yes."

"You have never yet tasted the quintes-
sential sweetness of a secret, my dear child,"

he said, with a lingering gaze, and throwing his arm lightly round his horse's neck.   " A secret, let me tell you, is a friend that never wearies you, a bosom friend that whispers to you in your hours of loneliness.   It makes society superfluous, books an intrusion, music the interruption of an inward harmony.   A secret is a kind of famulus or genius or fairy—what you will : it waves its wand, and an enchanted palace rises silent and lovely as the dawning of the day.   But when a secret is shared by two beings, it is the closest of all ties.   'Tis the chink between Pyramus and Thisbe.   Aha ! might I not be a poet of the Dellacruscan Academy ? If, therefore, you wish warmth in winter's cold, freshness in summer's heat — if you wish ' to sit i' the centre and enjoy bright day,' and carry an Italian sky about with you—then have some dainty delicious secret."

" It depends, I think, upon the secret," said Bell, venturing to look up with a smile. " But——"

" Ah ! you bring me back to prose ; and yet I thought my rhetoric was moving.   But it appears you are preoccupied with poor Prosser's concerns. My tirade has been wasted. Exit Holofernes."

"Indeed, my lord, it is always delightful to listen to you," said Bell.

"Thank you. But when you know me better you will say of me—

'In him much embryo, much abortion lay,
Much future ode, and abdicated play.'

What a wrench it is to leave you! Why cannot I lift you to my saddle-bow, and ride away, ride away to the land of Cockayne, or the gardens of Armida, or Arcadia, or Circe's Isle, or the Hesperides, or all in succession; for we have moods, passions, and delights suitable to each and all. I have made you blush, I vow. Forgive me. But as for this Prosser, I take it your intervention is pure friendship, is it not? It often happens that preceptors impart first the art of reading——"

"Oh, my lord, pray do not think——"

"I crave pardon again. I foresee you will have to be perpetually forgiving me, and I perpetually offending for the pleasure of being forgiven.   Adieu, my dear ward!"

He lifted her hand to his lips, smiled gaily, then swinging himself lightly into the saddle, rode off.

CHAPTER XII.

ANGER IN CELESTIAL MINDS.

As Bell trod her homeward way, her heart
beat lightly in her bosom. And yet she was
conscious of a feeling of abashed and incredu-
lous amazement. Who and what was she
that such a gentleman, so accomplished and
ingenious, should seem to take pleasure in
talking to her ? and should look at her so
winningly, and, she whispered to herself, so
fondly ? What did it mean ? Could it be
that this prince should stoop to such a Cinderella as she ? For even if her birth were
honourable, her manners and slender acquire-
ments were those of a Cinderella. But oh !
how sweet to be protected by such a man !
Such thoughts would come, rousing hot

blushes and a fever of the heart. But again, was he not apparently Sibylla's lover? And was it not disloyal to think of him save with dispassionate respect and distant admiration?

In her present mood she hoped she might not meet Sibylla. But, once more by the freakishness of fate, just as she was passing the lodge-gate of Beechgrove Hall, she beheld her friend coming down the avenue, adorably attired in a green sarcenet gown, with a dainty toque upon her head, and waving her green parasol as a signal to Bell that she was recognised.

Bell turned up the avenue to meet her friend.

"Oh thou faithless one," exclaimed Sibylla, shaking an admonitory finger, "you were passing the gate without coming to see me! Call you that backing your friends, turning your back upon them?"

"It is easily explained," said Bell. "I have had bad news, and I am very anxious to get back to Fownie as soon as possible."

" What news, my dearest dear ? "

" It appears that Mr Prosser is likely to be arrested."

" *La belle affaire!* Oh, I beg pardon. Why, yes; papa was telling me about that. Indeed, owing to Lord Wimpole's strong representation, papa was reluctantly induced to write out a warrant of arrest. But, in the first place, Mr Prosser seems to be a very incendiary sort of person, and a hatcher of sedition, who, as such, deserves little sympathy from you or me——"

" I know nothing of politics, but I know him to be a very excellent man, who has been constantly kind to me."

" What ! sits the wind in that quarter ? Is it possible that the heart which beats beneath that very becoming gown—did you make it yourself?"

" Every stitch, dear."

" What fairy fingers you have got ! Well, am I right ? "

" Right about what ? "

" That this excellent sedition - monger has inspired a virtuous attachment (that is the phrase, I believe) within my Celia's bosom ? "

" Oh, Sibylla, how wildly you do talk ! Workaday people have other things to think of than—love."

" Nay, I was but jesting, or rather giving utterance to a random conjecture. But where on earth have you been ? "

" I have left a letter at Swinton Hall, begging Lord Wimpole to interpose in Mr Prosser's behalf."

Sibylla frowned slightly, and looked suspiciously at her friend.

" You—went—to—Swinton—Hall ? " she asked, scanning the words.

" Yes, and wherefore not ? "

" It is a little unfortunate," replied Sibylla, with a sarcastic ring in her voice, " that both the gentlemen involved are unmarried. Believe me, however much our womanly sympathies may be excited, it is as dangerous to plead to one gentleman as it is to plead for another. Women, when they interfere, always complicate matters, for no one will believe that they interfere from disinterested motives. Nor do we, as a rule. I make allowance for your early training ; but surely, my dear child, you know that your visit to Swinton Hall was excessively improper."

"Improper!" exclaimed Bell, indignantly, for on such a theme the most dove-like maiden will angrily ruffle her feathers. "I protest, you take an undue advantage of your superior rank and age when you proceed to school me as to my behaviour. Let me tell you, I am to be judged not by appearance but by my motives."

"Oh, la, my dear child, motives are mixed ! and I surmise that there was a sprig of fancy in the plain woof of your errand."

"I vow there was none ; I am not so inflammable or so silly as some young ladies are."

"Young ladies, quotha ! Has your communication with a lord procured you this flattering denomination?"

"If to be ungenerous is to be a young lady, then, indeed, I am not one," said Bell.

"Madam, I crave your pardon," retorted Sibylla, making an elaborate curtsey.

" My time is too valuable, Miss Gordon, to be spent in the interchange of incivilities," said Bell, loftily, " so I shall even bid you good-day."

" What airs in the Maid of the Inn ! "

" I am not the Maid of the Inn, and your taunt is paltry."

" I do not indeed know what you are, any more than you do yourself," rejoined Sibylla, plying her poisoned arrows, " but it is certain you are vastly spoiled among your friends because you have a strawberry - and - cream complexion.   Nevertheless, it is a far cry from the Anchor Inn to Swinton Hall."

" I shall take care to remember that it is also a far cry from the Anchor Inn to Beech-grove Hall."

" You will do well, for I wish not Beech-grove Hall to be a half-way house."

" Madam, you are insolent," said Bell.

" Madam, you are a minx ! "

At this point both girls began to weep freely.

" You dear wretch ! " sobbed Sibylla, " you have wounded me to the heart."

"Oh, Sibylla," said Bell, in a broken voice, "you have spoken to me most cruelly."

"I confess I have," Sibylla replied; "but you provoked me by your perfidy."

"Perfidy? I understand you not, Sibylla."

"Is it not perfidy for a maiden to lie in ambush for her friend's lover?"

"Your language is intolerable, Miss Gordon," replied Bell, indignantly. "I lie in ambush? when it has been my constant endeavour to avoid Lord Wimpole."

"Hark you, Miss Simpson," said Sibylla, drawing herself up with an air of dignity which would have been slightly comical but for the passion that flashed in her eyes and quivered in her voice, "your avoidance of Lord Wimpole is itself suspicious. Your formal reserve when you have met him in my society has been too marked. When a maid puts on armour, it is a sign that she deems herself vulnerable. Nothing could be more proper, tantalisingly proper, than your behaviour; but the *sainte-nitouche*—I beg pardon, the sanctified prude—is ever the most dangerous of coquettes. When every look and tone say, 'Observe my coldness, sir,' they mean, 'Try to thaw me, thou teasingly impassive man!'"

Perhaps some of these envenomed darts struck home: at any rate Bell grew very pale, and though bitterly indignant, showed no vehemence in her reply.

"Very well, be it so, madam," she said, coldly. "I am your rival, it appears. Be it so, I say again."

"What! thou conceited chit!" cried Sibylla, laughing hysterically. "Do you think he would marry *you?* He might, perhaps —though I should hate him and you for it —take a short voyage with you to the island of Cythera——"

"Oh, shame, shame!" cried Bell; "where is your maiden modesty?" The two young women stood confronting each other with sparkling eyes and panting bosoms.

Then Sibylla threw up her arms, and burst into a passion of weeping.

"Oh, heaven help me!" she moaned. "But I have seen this coming. Oh, Bell, if I have wronged you, I implore your for-

giveness! And indeed I am half distraught.
It is my inward pain has made me inflict
pain. Nay, I know your goodness: it is
envy of it which has made me disparage it.
But my instincts are keen. I have detected
a subtle change in him and you. He was
coming to love me; his love was almost in
bloom, when a sudden frost came—no, not a
sudden frost, but the gradual chill which
creeps over a dying man. Nay, I blame
you not. I have been unjust, most likely,
and perchance you are as much a victim
as I; but I have not been so unjust as to
say or insinuate what is utterly groundless.
There is, there is a growing tenderness in
your heart which is giving fresh brightness
to your eyes, a softer bloom to your cheek,
a more elastic vigour to your limbs. Dare
you deny the change? Oh, my once fondly
loved companion, how cruel you have become!"

"I deny not the change, Sibylla," said
Bell, gently; "but you mistake the cause—
would that I could tell it you! But I have
promised secrecy, and I may not break my

vow. Oh, Sibylla, think of what would most delight me, conjecture it with all the ingenuity of your former affection, and then impute the change to that."

"Ah! I begin to understand," cried Sibylla, with parted lips, and a faint gleam of joy suffusing her agitated features. "You know something of your birth; you are not a nameless thing—ah! why did you not hint this before?"

"It is only a very short time ago that—but I must say no more; and what I have hinted must be revealed to no one. Have I your promise?"

"My most solemn promise. Oh, can you forgive me? Yet do not forgive me too readily, or I shall suspect again. Oh, this jealousy! this waking nightmare! this intermittent fever! Swear to me —— But I shall not make you swear, for I would only search your oath for some reservation, some evasion. Enough! let us part in peace. But if your birth be honourable, then your rivalry becomes possible. Oh God! that I should be so tossed to and fro.

Where is my self-respect, my pride? I understand everything now in human life— calamities, crimes, and even the exultant abandonment of virtue. Pity me, Bell! it is pitiful to make such an exhibition of my poor lacerated heart. Perhaps when I see you again, I shall be composed, and varnished over with a ladylike indifference and frivolity. But, ah! the pangs will still be there. And how you act shall determine whether I worship you as an angel or hate you as a demon. And now farewell," she said, with a strange blending of penitence and sternness.

She first held out her hand, and then, as if by an irresistible impulse, strained Bell to her heart. Bell submitted to the embrace with an inward feeling of revulsion. It seemed to her as if she were being bound by a vow of renunciation.

As she languidly retraced her steps towards Fownie, her mind recalled every phase of the agitating interview with a vivid intensity that wearied her. This outburst of passion was a revelation to her. Were the poets and dramatists, then, right when they

depicted the fierce excess, the feverish long-
ings, of love? Were the people who ate and
drank and went to market subject to such
overmastering emotions? If so, what unseen tragedies were being enacted every-
where! The casual smile proceeded often,
perchance, from some inward illumination,
some brooding ecstasy; the clouded look for
which a trivial cause suggested itself was
often, perhaps, the expression of a hopeless
sorrow. Was it indeed true that every
man liveth to himself, and holds a com-
munion with himself which in the very
bustle of resort implies an utter loneliness?

Then several things which Sibylla had
said burned in her memory, and caused a
feeling of almost physical pain and disgust.
She felt degraded and debased when she
thought of them. Never could she forget
or forgive that hint about "a short voyage to
the island of Cythera." It seemed to poison
the very springs of feeling. It smirched the
pure soft feathers of Venus' doves. And yet,
perhaps, the leering innuendo was useful.
The ignorance which is prized in woman is

often fatal to her; and perchance the half-discovered mystery of evil is more appalling and more deterrent than its crude deformity.

By the time Bell had reached Fownie, Andrew had already taken his departure. He carried a small bag slung over his shoulder, and held a stout staff in his hand. It was a lovely evening, with a wide sweep of overarching blue flecked with strips and wisps of cloud lazily trailing and feathering out in the upper regions of the atmosphere. The air was cool and sweet, a pure benison to wearied lungs.

Andrew beguiled the monotony of his solitary march by repeating those odes of Horace which were his special favourites. He had finished the ode beginning "Quid fles, Asterie," and the thoughts and feelings suggested by it occupied his mind for a considerable time.

"It's a bonnie name 'Asterie,'" he ruminated; "and, indeed, every good and lovely maiden is like a star. Ah, Milly, shall I ever forget your starry eyes? That's no very likely, is it? But it's no likely either

that I'll ever return blessed with Bithynian
merchandise.   There's only one thing likely,
and that is that I'll hae to 'spend the sleep-
less nights not without many tears.'   Well,
it's a rueful comfort that I dinna need to tell
her, 'Abide unyielding' to another suitor;
for I'm sure she likes the puir blundering
dominie too much, unworthy though he be,
to listen to any other man's tale of love.
Can anything in this world of change be as
grand as constancy?   It is the law of nature,
it is the glory of God Himself, with whom
'is no variableness, neither shadow of turning.'   But indeed, when a man has won
such a woman's heart, there's little credit in
constancy.   When a man really loves the
Bible or Shakespeare, he will never cast
them aside for another book; and she's my
Bible and my Shakespeare bound together,
for indeed her looks are 'gospel books,' and
I find her in every one of Shakespeare's
lovely creations."

His sentimental musings were interrupted
by the rumble of a distant vehicle behind
him.

He had now accomplished half the intervening distance, and the road at this stage of his journey passed through a wood which, forming a canopy of foliage above, seemed to anticipate the shades of night. The sounds increased rapidly in distinctness, and he could distinguish the trot of a pair of horses. He was not a timid man, and he was a proud man to boot, nevertheless he felt vaguely alarmed. And he had cause for anxiety, for in an inside pocket of his bag he had the minutes of the last Chapter of the Knight-Templars, and a considerable number of dangerous documents, with not a few specimens of French revolutionary literature. He stood still and looked back, waiting till the vehicle came in sight. It seemed a lumbering family-coach, but was evidently drawn by two powerful and spirited animals. Two men were seated on the box, and as he stood gazing, a head was protruded from the window and seemed to reconnoitre the route. The coach came on and passed him, and Andrew heaved a sigh of relief; but his satisfaction was of short duration. The horses were abruptly pulled up, the door was opened, and a short but wiry-looking man sprang into the road, followed by John Wilkie.

The first individual halted in the middle of the road and drew a paper out of his pocket. He wore a broad blue bonnet, a coarse cloth jacket of the same colour, and velveteen breeches reaching a little below the knee. Andrew recognised him at once as Saunders, the town-officer of St Thomas.

This official having peremptorily ordered Andrew to stand still, proceeded to read the document which he held in his hand. It ran as follows :—

" I, Matthew Gordon, Justice of the Peace in the County of Forfar, do hereby empower William Saunders, Town-officer of St Thomas, to arrest and lodge in the Town-house of St Thomas, Andrew Prosser, Schoolmaster of Fownie, on well-grounded suspicion of treason and disaffection to the Government. Given at my house of Beechgrove, the twenty-fifth day of May, seventeen hundred and ninety-four, under my hand and seal. Matthew Gordon, J.P."

"Now, Andrew Prosser," said Saunders, "I summon you to surrender yourself into my custody."

Andrew hesitated for a moment or two. It was tolerably certain that if he were arrested he would be searched, and if so the compromising documents in his possession would furnish abundant materials for an indictment of treason before the Court of Justiciary. In that case, his political associates would be equally involved in ruin. A man thinks rapidly in such emergencies, and on a hurried survey of the consequences likely to follow from his apprehension, he resolved to resist capture.

"I refuse to give myself up," he said, curtly.

"Ye misguided loon," cried Saunders, "dae ye ken what deforcement of the officers of the law means?"

"I ken that there's ower muckle law and ower little justice in puir Scotland at this present," said Andrew, bitterly.

At this crisis John Wilkie interposed.

"Andrew, gie yoursel' up peaceably," he

said, a little remorsefully. " It's nae shame
to you to strike your colours when you're
outnumbered. I would be wae to board a
fine lad like you; but duty, ye ken—we
maun a' jump to the bosun's whistle."

"I have my duty as well," said Andrew,
resolutely. "And I give you fair warning,
all of you, that I'll defend myself. Dinna
blame me, John Wilkie, if ye get a few
clours."

"Clours come natural to me, Andrew,
baith in the giving and receiving," said
John, stoutly. "Ye had better clap a stopper
on that lang tongue o' yours, and come aboard
this craft handsomely," and he pointed to the
coach.

Saunders, seeing that Andrew had put
himself in a posture of defence, and measur-
ing his antagonist's strength with professional accuracy, hung in the wind, as John
Wilkie might have said.

"Are ye afraid, ye lubber ?" cried Wilkie,
indignantly. "If I hadna a jury-mast o' a
leg, I wouldna stand here like a jack-tar
whistling for a wind."

"You're a bold British tar, John," said Andrew, mockingly, "attacking me with a cutlass when I have only a bit stick. Put that in your pipe, John, and smoke it."

"Cutlash be ——," growled Wilkie, sheathing his weapon, however, with an awkwardly shamefaced air. "Come doon frae the box, Sandy, and gie us a hand." At the same time the driver descended and went to the horses' heads, in case the animals should be rendered restive by the impending struggle.

The town-officer, feeling his reputation at stake, now clutched firmly the stout staff with which he was armed, and advanced to the attack, while Wilkie took off the broad leathern belt that encircled his waist, and swinging it round his head, stumped up towards Andrew. Before, however, he could deliver a blow, Saunders had received a stroke on his right arm that made him drop his weapon with a howl of rage and pain. The next instant the buckle of Wilkie's belt descended with merciless vigour on Andrew's head, stunning him for a few moments. The old tar then grappled with his antagonist.

The man who had been hailed as Sandy followed his example, and a violent struggle ensued, in the course of which Andrew's wallet was torn from him, and he was severely mauled by Wilkie's formidable fists. Andrew, even in his excitement and exasperation, forbore to take full advantage of his muscular strength against the old sailor; but a fortunate kick shivered the wooden leg, and Wilkie, after pirouetting for a second or two, went by the board, as he might have said, and measured his length on the ground. Relieved of one assailant, Andrew clutched the other by the throat and drove his head against a tree with a shock that made the teeth rattle in his head. Saunders meanwhile was dancing about nursing his injured arm and swearing copiously. Andrew now sprang into the middle of the road and rushed towards the driver, who, seeing his approach, slunk away from the horses' heads. In another moment Andrew had clambered up to the box, seized the reins, and whipping up the plunging and excited animals, drove off at a furious pace.

CHAPTER XIII.

LORD WIMPOLE PLAYS THE PART OF THE GOOD SAMARITAN.

FOR a considerable time, as may be supposed, Andrew could do nothing more than hold the reins and guide the horses; but when he recovered his breath and some measure of composure, he perceived the serious difficulties in which he had involved himself. He must be ready with an explanation of the plight he was in; some plausible tale must be concocted. He surveyed himself ruefully. He had lost his bonnet in the tussle, his coat was rent, and one sleeve hung by a few stitches. His face also bore witness of hard usage, one eye was nearly closed, his upper lip cut, his knuckles skinned, and a fiery red stripe ran across his cheek where Wilkie's belt had struck him. His first resolve was to leave the horses and vehicle somewhere in the neighbourhood of Dundee, and enter the town on foot. But even then his appearance would excite comment and suspicion.

He accordingly determined to state that, having dropped his whip, he had descended from the box, and that on his attempting to remount, the horses had bolted and had dragged him some distance along the ground as he clung to the reins. He had been sent to fetch a doctor for Lord Wimpole, who was ill with a fever. Such was the groundwork of his explanation, and he employed the rest of his time in anticipating objections and embarrassing questions, and in giving a general solidity and coherence of parts to his airy fabric. It is impossible to tell how much hard lying a man is capable of, till the emergency arises. Andrew even derived a species of grim amusement from the elaboration of his fictions, and with a kind of artistic prodigality he lavished upon the fruit of his imagination a number of flourishes and decorative designs.

Having his story pat and proof against incredulity, as he thought, he set himself squarely in his seat, brandished his whip with a professional air, and apostrophised the horses with names, at which they pricked their ears in astonishment, but with resignation, for they appreciated his power of wrist, and respected his application of the whip. Darkness was setting in when he reached Dundee. He drove up the Nethergate to the Black Bull Inn. The landlord came to the door and gazed at driver and equipage with silent stupefaction. An ostler in his shirt-sleeves emerged from the yard, chewing a meditative straw, and fell into a cataleptic state. A number of loungers —for every inn harbours such parasites— gathered as if at a signal, and leaning against the walls, added their quota of wondering scrutiny.

"Here, my man," said Andrew sharply to the ostler, "dinna stand glowerin' at me. Unyoke the horses and bait them

while I gang for a doctor;" and so saying
he dismounted as rapidly as his stiff and
aching limbs permitted.

"A doctor?" repeated the landlord, rousing himself from depths of mystified speculation. "What's wrang?"

"I hae little time to stand palavering,"
said Andrew, impatiently. "Lord Wimpole
wouldna thank me for haverin' while he
was groaning."

"Lord Wimpole of Swinton Ha'? Is he
took ill?"

"Fever, they think," said Andrew, with
a rueful shake of the head. "Or maybe
small - pox," he added, with portentous
solemnity.

The landlord edged away into the passage,
and shouted to the ostler, "Take the horses
in, ye muckle gomeral, and be quick aboot it."

The ostler growled some inarticulate reply,
and, as he unbuckled the straps, said to
Andrew—

"Ye wouldna be the waur o' a doctor
yoursel', I'm thinkin'. Where did ye get
a' thae clours?"

"I canna manage horses as well as you, my braw lad," said Andrew, with a shrug. "I hae had a sair ca'-through with the beasties. First they bolted when I was getting up—I had dropped my whip, ye see—and I found myself whummlin' along the road like a poke o' draff, but holding the reins like grim death: it's a mercy I didna get among the wheels. Then when I did get to my feet—there was a providential rise in the road and they slackened their pace a bit, and sma' wonder wi' sic a Noah's Ark at their heels—I had a sair ado to get up to the box. Even then I wasna at the end o' my tribulations, for sic reesty beasts I never saw: if I hadna held the reins firm, they would hae been at the back o' beyont by this time — ye ugly deevils!" and he shook his fist at the unoffending animals.

"They look canny enough," said the ostler.

"They may weel be that. I hae ta'en the spunk oot o' them, I'se warrant."

"Ye've trashed them sair, that's positive,"

said the ostler. "Ye're no used to horses, I'll wager."

"Me! I would almost as soon ride ahint a witch on a broom-stick; but his lordship's coachman has the rheumatism, and I couldna refuse. But I'll send in a lang bill for sticking-plaster," he added, with a significant laugh. "Dinna gie them ower muckle aits, or Jehu himsel' wouldna be fit to drive them. I'll be back in the course of an hour wi' a doctor."

"'Od man, ye'll founder them!" said the ostler, with professional concern.

"Let them founder!" exclaimed Andrew, impatiently. "What's that to Lord Wimpole's life?"

Andrew turned away, and at the same moment caught sight of Lord Wimpole riding hastily down the street towards the inn. Andrew's heart gave a violent throb, and then seemed to stop beating.

"It's a' ower wi' me," he muttered faintly; "and serve me right for telling sic a lot o' cracks."

Escape was impossible, for Lord Wimpole's

keen eye had espied him at once, and Andrew interpreted too well the sardonic smile on his enemy's dark features.

Andrew went forward to him, and said calmly—

"Do with me as you please, my lord. 'Conclamatum est.'"

Lord Wimpole laughed, and playfully tapped him on the shoulder with his whip.

"Would it embarrass you, Mr Prosser, if I dismounted at the Black Bull?" he asked, with almost a roguish smile.

"Indeed it would," said Andrew, bluntly. "I have been reeling off lies by the fathom."

"It only needs a beginning, Mr Prosser. Telling lies, as you ingenuously call it, is the labour of the Danaïdes. Well, it would be a pity to wither the first blossoms of your imagination. Oblige me by accompanying me to the Royal George. I have something to say to you."

Andrew acquiesced with a bow, and marched along towards the Royal George with the calmness and even the indifference of despair. Reaching the inn, Lord Wimpole consigned his horse to the care of an ostler, and entering bespoke a private room, at the same time ordering refreshments for two. The landlord having surveyed Andrew with frowning astonishment, Lord Wimpole said curtly, "See if you can procure a presentable coat and hat for my companion. He has met with an accident."

Andrew made no comment; indeed if Lord Wimpole had ordered a roc's egg he would hardly have expressed surprise.

. "Now, Mr Prosser, sit down, if you please," said his lordship, with a grim but not unkindly smile. "After having slain the Philistines hip and thigh with a great slaughter, and, to alter the historical perspective, having sped along the Flaminian Way with your glowing axle, you must need rest and refreshment."

"My lord, it is hardly generous to season your revenge with this irony of kindness. It is a dreary and Saturnine kind of humour."

"Mr Prosser, I design nothing against you," said Lord Wimpole, gravely. "Nay more, I am here to help you in your present predicament."

Andrew stared at him incredulously, and then laid his head upon the table to hide the outburst of emotion which overmastered him.

"Compose yourself," said Lord Wimpole. "The waiter will be here presently with refreshments."

Andrew rose, and stepping to the window, looked out upon the street, while his companion sat silent, thoughtfully tapping his boot with his whip.

A noble round of beef and a couple of bottles of claret were brought in by a deferential waiter. When he had arranged the table and softly withdrawn, Lord Wimpole turned round.

"Now, Mr Prosser, pray join me at this extemporary refection."

"Your lordship heaps coals of fire on my head," said Andrew, brokenly.

"Not a jot, not a jot, except it be the luxury of revenge to feed your enemy. Here is claret, if I mistake not, that would 'create a soul under the ribs of death.' It is astonishing how eating and drinking change our horizon. Your good health, Mr Prosser!"

"My humble duty to your lordship," said Andrew, chokingly.

But when he saw his plate piled with honest beef, which was variegated with cunning streaks of red and white, most movingly appealing to the palate, he straightway felt ravenous, and fell to with right good will. The claret too, with its rounded and velvety caressing upon his tongue, diffused comfort through his wearied body, and his stomach felt a gratitude that its neighbour the heart is often too chary of confessing. In brief, he made a Gargantuan meal, and his companion worthily emulated his prowess.

"Now, sir," said Andrew, with a laugh, and drawing a full breath to gauge with satisfaction the full measure of his repletion, "I feel as if I could fight with wild beasts at Ephesus. But may I ask what your lordship means by this? for 'tis clean out of my reckoning."

"The matter is simple. A mutual friend has pled on your behalf——"

"Miss Bell?" asked Andrew, eagerly.

Lord Wimpole nodded.

"It's like her," said Andrew. "There's nothing but kindness and truth and fidelity in that angel-bosom."

Lord Wimpole thrust forth his hand and gripped Andrew's so vigorously that he winced.

"You have rightly described her," he said, in deep thrilling tones. "Now to business; we must not be discursive on such a theme. I suppose you are in a bad fix?"

"I'm a ruined man, my lord."

"So bad?"

"Yes; they've got my wallet, and there's enough in it to hang or transport me."

"You have me to thank for that, I fear."

"Well, your lordship is what the school-men call the proximate cause, but you have only anticipated what was sure to happen."

"You must flee the country, I suppose."

"That I will, this very night," said Andrew.

"I shall not detain you at such a time. You will have arrangements to make, and time is precious. Now, Mr Prosser, there are few ills in life that are not alleviated by a little money, and I have come provided for this emergency. Pray, hear me out. I propose to lend you a trifle, which you can repay in more fortunate circumstances."

"That means the Greek calends, my lord. I could not——"

"'Tis no matter. I do nothing by halves. Our mutual friend will be distressed if you show any mistaken delicacy at such a crisis of your fortunes. Here is a leather-bag, which you will, I hope, guard more carefully than you did your political grenade, which has now, I fear, burst. As Miss Bell's friend, you must be mine. Take it with my hearty good wishes."

Andrew took the bag proffered him, his manly features convulsed with irrepressible emotion.

"This is kind, this is generous, this is divine," he faltered. "How small I am beside your lordship! Forgive me all my hard thoughts of you. Oh, why do you hide that bright and heavenly light of your nature under a bushel?"

Lord Wimpole blenched, and his features assumed almost a harrowed look.

"Say no more—you little know me, Mr Prosser. But if *she* trusts me——" He sighed heavily.

"She does, she must," exclaimed Andrew, eagerly. "Ah, my lord, you have a strange fascination. Use it for good. Be kind to women, who, alas! have often to fight against their own hearts as well as against the world. Resist yourself, if they cannot resist you. I understand it now. I would fight for you to my last breath. Oh, my lord, be always as noble as you so often are!" and seizing Lord Wimpole's hand, he pressed it to his own labouring heart.

"We grow elegiac," said Lord Wimpole, with a catch in his voice. "Enough of this! Now, farewell! Lose no time in making preparations for flight. And if you are ever in serious straits, write to me. I shall send the waiter up with some articles of apparel. Farewell."

So saying, he hurriedly left the room.

"Now this is a lesson to me never to judge," said Andrew solemnly to himself. "I see now how it is that our heavenly Father is so long-suffering. He kens what is good in a' His puir erring creatures, and He doesna need to be in a hurry. That fine man has doubtless often grieved the Spirit of Grace, but he'll be forgiven, that he will, because he loved much. And to think that my wee bonnie Bell can row him round her finger! Hoots! she's just his guardian angel in a tenement of clay. She will ransom him for goodness. I hope it isna irreverence to think that if there had been women-angels in heaven, as there are on earth, puir auld Clootie wouldna hae fallen."

Ten minutes later Andrew stepped resolutely out of the inn. His first visit was to the Abbot of the Chapter of Knight-Templars. This worthy, who had acted as master of ceremonies at the initiation of Simpson, was a bird-fancier. Andrew found

him engaged in stuffing a mallard, and at
once gave him a succinct account of his
recent adventures. The Abbot received the
intelligence of the loss of the wallet and its
incriminating contents with profound con-
sternation, and rated Andrew soundly on
his want of prudence.

"Ay, ay," said Andrew, bitterly. "Kick
a man when he's down. But ye needna be
sae carfuffled. What can the authorities
make of Brother Bernardus, and Anastasius,
and the like? There isna a proper name in
the whole minute-book."

"That's true," remarked the Abbot, considerably reassured. "What do you mean
to do?"

"Well, ye see, there was a hantle o' documents, newspapers, pamphlets, and so on,
that are quite enough to settle my case.
I must flee the country."

"It would doubtless be the best plan,"
said the Abbot.

"Ay, ay—'calca Cæsaris hostem,'" said
Andrew, sarcastically. "I'll be outlawed,
mind you. I may never see Auld Scot-

land again.   I never thought I loved it
so much."

"Brother Ludovic sails to-night," said the
Abbot, eagerly.

"Where is he bound?"

"For France."

"In the way of fair trade, I suppose?"

"So I suppose—he is bound for Boulogne."

"Can ye get me on board?"

"Easily."

"Come along then, and arrange the affair
with him."

The Abbot gave an embarrassed cough.

"It's rather unchancy for the two of
us——"

"Oh, I see," said Andrew, caustically.
"I'm a social leper now.   Unclean! unclean!"

"Prudence is the handmaid of safety,"
remarked the Abbot, pompously.

"Prudence is cousin-german to cowardice,
I'm thinking," Andrew retorted.

"I'll give you a line for Brother Ludovic," said the Abbot, soothingly.

"You'll give me line enough to let me swing, I'se warrant."

"You are excited and unreasonable," said the Abbot, with his official air of dignity.

"I'm no excited — I'm scunnered!" said Andrew, indignantly. "*You* struggle for liberty! *You* lead the People into the Promised Land! Na, na; stuff your wrens and your tomtits—that's *your* vocation. Well, give me the line and let me go."

"I'll give you your line," said the Abbot, disdainfully. "But I shall report your language to the Chapter."

"Ye can repeat it to the whole Canon," retorted Andrew, "including the Apocrypha; but for any sake leave out the Maccabees, for you hae nothing in common with the brave Hebrew patriots."

The Abbot in great haste scrawled a few lines on a scrap of paper, which he handed to Andrew with an absurd attempt at dignity. Andrew scanned it rapidly, and put it in his pocket.

"I would not advise you," he said, "to

hold a Chapter in a hurry. There seems
to be treachery somewhere. You had better
revise your Chapter; I think a corrupt reading has got into it."

So saying, and with a contemptuous smile
on his lips, he left the apartment, and made
his way in hot haste to his Aunt Jane's shop.

When Andrew appeared before his aunt,
she held up her hands in dismay.

"Be gracious to us, Andrew! what hae
ye been after? Why, ye're a' wounds and
bruises and purifying sores!"

"I hae had a bit tuilzie. Never mind
that. I'm in a hurry. Ye see, I must run
the country."

"Ay, ay, I thought it would come to
this," said Aunt Jane, with considerable
equanimity. "Weel, we a' hae oor tribulations. Many a time I am weary o' my
groaning, as the Psalmist says, though I
question if he suffered as much as I do.
Last night——"

"Ye can catalogue your ailments another
time, auntie. I'm in a hurry."

"Ye're aye in a hurry," retorted Aunt

Jane, with an indignant sniff. "However, gang your ways. Ye were aye wise in your ain conceit."

"I hae tried to make the world better than I found it. I'm no the first man that has found the Auld Adam ower strong for him."

"It doesna do, Andrew, to be keekin' into everybody's kail-pot. Ye'll no get thanks for that."

"Well, I'm no here to argle-bargle. Can you give me a morsel of writing-paper? I hae a letter to write."

After considerable delay he was provided with writing materials, and sitting down he scrawled a few lines of hearty thanks to Bell for her kind interposition on his behalf, at the same time stating his obligations to Lord Wimpole in the warmest and most effusive terms.

"You'll get this posted for me, auntie?" he said, when he had carefully wafered his letter.

"Oh yes, I'll dae that for you, Andrew," said Aunt Jane, magnanimously.

" Well, good-bye, auntie," said Andrew. " Ye've got rid of a ne'er-do-well for a while."

" Good-bye, Andrew. I hope your afflic-tions will be blest to you."

" Thank you," said Andrew, with a rueful grimace, as he hastily withdrew.

A rapid walk of ten minutes took him to the harbour. This harbour occupied but a contracted space, and was enclosed by a rough, crooked, and misshapen breast-work of stone, extended on one side so as to form a small pier or jetty. At that time the trade in various kinds of linen fabrics gave employment during the year to not much more than a hundred vessels of very moder-ate tonnage. It was quite dark as Andrew went down to the Sea-gate, and there was a fog upon the water. A lantern suspended from the foremast of a lugger guided his steps to the place where the vessel lay. It was of about fifty tons burthen, was decked, and had two masts and a running jib-boom. Andrew, on coming alongside, hailed a sea-man who was lolling over the bulwark.

" Where's the skipper ? "

The sailor replied with an oath that he did not know, adding the conviction, however, that the skipper was stowing liquor in his hold.

Further inquiry was rendered unnecessary by the somewhat lurching approach of an enormously stout man, wearing jack-boots, a pea-jacket, and a sou'-wester. He was followed at a respectful distance by a group of half-a-dozen seamen. This individual Andrew recognised at once as Brother Ludovic, and going up to him he said in a whisper, "When is lint in the bell ? "

Brother Ludovic started slightly, and peered suspiciously into Andrew's face.

" That depends on the weather," he replied, and then added heartily, " Oh, it's you, Andrew. Glad to see you. Come on board, and bowse up your jib."

" Drinking is no in my mind at present," said Andrew, gloomily. " But I'll come on board, for I hae weighty things to tell you."

" Ye seem dowie-like, but a tot of grog

will hearten you up," said the skipper, whose name was Michael Burnside.

So saying, he swung himself on board and squeezed himself down the companion into his little cabin, followed by Andrew.

A swinging lamp dimly lighted the tiny apartment, and Michael's big body seemed by force of contrast almost colossal.

He straightway lifted the lid of a locker, and taking out a bottle of rum, poured a liberal quantity into two large glasses.

"Now, Andrew, overhaul your log, but dinna pay out mair slack than ye can help, for the tide's making fast."

Andrew accordingly gave a brief account of his present circumstances, and concluded by inquiring whether Michael would take him on board, and land him at Boulogne, adding that he was able and willing to pay for his passage.

"Hoots! ye'll be handy in working the ship; and tarry breeks gang free, ye ken. But what will ye dae in France? Things are a' tapsalteery there, as I hear."

"God knows! But I'm thinking I could

maybe get out to America from Havre or
Bordeaux, and then I could make my living
easy. I'm a fair seaman, having had to do
with boats since I was a boy; and if I canna
get teaching, or clerking, or work in a store,
I'll e'en try the coasting-trade."

"Hae ye shot in the locker? For ye
needna gang to America withoot that. If
ye want to get on wi' the Yankees, ye must
be able to birl the bawbees. They're a
grippy lot, and would buy you, and then
sell you at the next market. Naething for
naething, says Jonathan."

"I am fairly well provided, thanks to a
generous friend."

"Say the word, and I'll lend you fifty
pounds," said Michael, who was in a mellow
state of mind.

"You're a true friend, Michael," said
Andrew, tremulously. "And I'll never
forget your kindness."

"Avast there!" said the skipper, smiting
the table with his ponderous fist. "Belay
all that nonsense, Andy. Besides, we are
bound to help you. We're an Associated

Order — though, mind you, there's some I dinna care a dottle for. There's the Abbot. His tongue works like a loose fid; but when it comes to doing, it's up keeleg and run, or I'm mista'en. There's mair canvas than cargo aboot him."

Andrew shook his head significantly.

"He gave me a bit line for you, Michael."

"Did he, though? Light your pipe wi' it, Andy. I need nae lines. You're here, and ye're welcome. Confound his impudence! Does he think he's commodore to gie me my sailing orders?" and Michael spat contemptuously on the floor.

Andrew's self-command had been so severely tried by the agitations of the day that the seaman's bluff kindness entirely unmanned him. He laid his head on the table to hide his emotion.

"Avast there!" cried the skipper in his stentorian voice, and slapping Andrew vigorously on the shoulders. "Will ye pipe your eye like a sailor's sweetheart when she's bundled into the shore-boat? Be a man!"

"I'm a broken man, Michael," said Andrew,

with a groan. "I must leave my home, my country, my——"

The skipper hastily took a mouthful of grog, half choked himself, and coughed till his large face seemed distended to the bursting-point. After relieving himself with a volley of full-flavoured oaths, he cried out, "Do ye think that I'm to waste my time preaching to you, and pulling lang faces like a loblolly boy? Avast! ye're no the first braw lad that has had to cut his cable and run."

"It's over," said Andrew, breathing heavily. "Something went round my heart, but it's over."

"Take a dram, Andy," said the skipper, cheerfully. "That's the richt medicine for a sick heart. I mind when Jean Armstrong threw me ower. She said there was ower muckle o' me to take at ae gulp. She married a peelie-walie 'pothecary lad afterhin, serve her richt! Eh, but I was bad for a while, for she was a bonnie lassie. I mind the glint o' her een yet, the gilpy! What would I hae been then withoot a stiff dram?

I tried Hollands and Jamaica and Cognac,
but I aye seemed to hear her say, as she
often said, puir lassie, ' Ca' canny, Michael.'
Weel, weel, she's in her grave lang syne."

He heaved a portentous sigh, and rose to
his feet, saying, "I must see what the ram-
paging deevils are after. It's aboot time we
were aff. We'll hae to use our sweeps, I'm
thinking."

Much stamping of feet on the deck now
followed, and the skipper's oaths pervaded
the atmosphere. Ere long Andrew heard
the cry of " Cast off," and the lugger began
to move, propelled by boat-hooks from the
pier. Once in the tide-way the sails were
hoisted. Andrew went on deck, and leaning
against the bulwarks, gazed long and wistfully
at the lights of the town. But as the wind
was light and baffling, the sweeps were got
out, and Andrew, glad to divert his mind
from saddening reflections, lent a hand. An
hour passed, by which time they were near-
ing the mouth of the Firth, and the breeze,
which had come and gone in languid puffs
like a sick man's laboured but feeble breath-

ing, now began to blow with steadier volume.
Long lines of white water gleamed spectrally
on Barrie sands. The sweeps were taken in,
and the lugger began to forge ahead under
foresail, mainsail, and jib. Andrew joined the
skipper, who was standing by the wheel,
every now and then "squinting" at the sky
overhead. The fog had lifted, and patches
of cloud were floating across the moon, their
edges ravelled out in vapoury fringes and
filaments, which showed a disposition to part
from the denser masses, as if the wind were
increasing in strength in the upper regions of
the atmosphere.

"Boreas is picking the wool aff his lambs,"
said Michael, with a laugh. "We'll hae the
shearing ere lang. Keep her at that, Sandy,
east and by north, till I gie ye the word."

"Ay, ay, sir," said the helmsman.

The skipper now descended to his cabin,
inviting Andrew to accompany him.

CHAPTER XIV.

MRS BADGER HAS AN OBJECTIONABLE VISITOR.

ANDREW'S non-appearance on the following day caused great commotion and excitement in Fownie; but in the course of the forenoon the news spread of his attempted capture, and of its failure owing to his stubborn and desperate resistance. As opposition to the law was thoroughly congenial to the spirit of the community, Andrew's popularity took at once an upward bound; and had he returned, he would doubtless have been received with a triumphal demonstration. But two or three days passed without any intelligence respecting his fate, and his friends and acquaintances came to the unwilling conclusion that he had "run the country."

Mrs Badger was in a state of sore affliction; for despite the harsh surface of her nature, she had a feeling heart, and was secretly much attached to Andrew. She had indeed no hesitation in painting his defects in vivid colours with a Biblical brush, but she only exhibited the portraiture to himself, and deep in her heart she acknowledged the sincerity, manly courage, and unpretending kindness of his nature.

His disappearance, therefore, made a sad blank in her otherwise monotonous existence. She missed his pungent though never acrimonious sarcasm, the raspiness and snarl of his discontented and aggressive fiddle, which, sooth to say, was of plebeian origin, and had much of the peevishness of youth; she missed the wreaths of smoke from his long clay pipe, which she did not fail to dust carefully, and replace on the mantelpiece with a heavy sigh; she missed, perhaps most of all, the little skirmishes which gave a dramatic interest to her life.

She would sit for hours on a "creepie" reading her Bible, sighing over the Lamentations of Jeremiah or following the vicissitudes of David's career after he was banished from the court of Saul and took to the hills as a magnanimous bandit.

On Monday of the following week she was busily engaged polishing the mahogany table of the little parlour, occasionally moistening its surface with a few pious drops, when a peremptory knock came to the door. Her heart gave a responsive throb, and she almost flew to the door. On opening it, a strange-looking personage met her gaze. This unexpected visitor was a short ill-favoured man, enveloped in a long overcoat which flapped round his attenuated limbs, and was "sicklied o'er" with the greenish shimmer of age. Its greasy cuffs almost concealed a pair of meagre and very dirty hands, the curved fingers of which were tipped with long black-rimmed nails so as to present an uncomfortable resemblance to talons. He had a large loose mouth, and the wiry tufts

of a straggling moustache imperfectly concealed two front teeth of inordinate size.
His eyes were keen and restless, at once
cowering and lowering in expression, while
his features were perked up with a laboured
affectation of impudent importance.

"Ye'll ken me again, mistress," he said,
somewhat abashed by her severe and evidently unfavourable scrutiny.

"Folks that ken ye ance, dinna want
to ken ye a second time, I'se warrant,"
retorted Mrs Badger. "Who may ye be?"

"I'm mair in the habit o' speirin' than
answering," he replied, with a grotesque
attempt to assume a dignified air. "Is
Andrew Prosser in?"

"No, he's no in," she replied, with much
asperity; "and if he was, he wouldna hae
dealings wi' a cheat-the-woodie like you.
Gang your gait. There's nae charity here
for wastrels."

"Stash your gab," blurted out the fellow,
hotly, "ye auld cankered carline. I'm a
messenger-at-arms."

"Ye're fit for the job," retorted Mrs

Badger, caustically. "And what may ye be wantin'?"

"Let me in; I hae to search the hoose," he said.

"I'll dae that. I can aye burn some flowers o' sulphur afterhin. But wipe your dirty shoon on the mat," she added, with an emphasis that included his whole person in the recommendation.

He sulkily complied, and entering the house, made a minute investigation, accompanied by Mrs Badger, who enlivened his occupation with sarcastic comments and ironical advice.

"Eh, but ye're a fell woman," he remarked when his perquisition was concluded. "Ye hae an ill-scraped tongue, guid wife; and I'm thinkin' I hae got Andrew's portion as weel as my ain. Weel, weel, hard names break nae banes. As for Andrew, he's fugitate, that's clear."

"What's fugitate? Dinna talk thieves' Latin to me, gin ye please."

"Fugitate? Andrew kens brawly what that means, I trow. He has fled from the authority o' the law, that's what it means. In a way, that saves the law a lot o' trouble, for after a judgment of outlawry has been pronounced, his life isna worth a docken. Anybody can kill him if he resists capture, and nae guilt is incurred."

"And what is he charged with?" asked Mrs Badger in a somewhat tremulous voice.

"Treason!" replied the messenger - at - arms with pompous relish. "I hold a warrant for his apprehension from the Sheriff of Forfar in pursuance of a writ of Capias from the High Court of Justiciary.

"What's likely to happen, now that Andrew has fled?" asked Mrs Badger, her anxiety dominating every other feeling.

"Weel, as ye've gotten off your high horse, I'll e'en tell ye," said the messenger, not averse to show his importance as an oracle of the law. "But hae ye got a mouthful o' spirits aboot the hoose? I'm sair forfoughten wi' my lang walk."

"I'll gie you a dram afore ye gang awa'," said Mrs Badger, severely. "Ill be bound,

folks are mair willing to gie you a deoch-an-
doruis than a propine."

"Aweel, I dinna invite mysel'. But I'll
answer your question. First of all, a Writ
of Proclamation will be issued, whereby
Prosser will be proclaimed three times—ance
at the Sheriff Court, a second time at the
Quarter Sessions, and the third time near
the door o' the Parish Kirk. If he is still
latitate—that is, in hiding—a Writ o' Exi-
gent will be issued, calling him to appear
and surrender himself at ane or other of five
successive Courts—the law gies him a lang
rope, but ilka time he fails to appear it's
another coil roond his neck. If he doesna
appear at any o' these Courts, judgment
of Outlawry is pronounced. He is then a
fugitive and a vagabond on the face o' the
earth; civilly he's a dead man; he has
nae mair richts than a kittiwake. So, if
ye ken where he is——"

"But I dinna," protested Mrs Badger,
humbly, being completely overawed by this
formidable recital of legal proceedings.

"A man doesna slip away from his friends

like a knotless threed," said the messenger, shaking his head. "And mind, compounding of felony is a serious matter. However, I hae warned ye," and he passed his hand significantly over his lips.

Mrs Badger went into the house and returned with a bottle of whisky and a glass.

"Help yersel'," she said, shortly. "'Wine is a mocker, strong drink is raging.'"

"Very true, mistress, wine *is* a mocker. Ye may take a hale bottle o' claret and no feel even a bummin' in your heid. My respects!"

So saying he quaffed his glass, and handing it back with a wistful look, took his departure.

An hour later, Mrs Badger was rapping at the manse door. It cost her a great effort to take this step; but she was in sore perplexity, and felt the need of advice.

She was ushered into the parlour, where she found the minister and his wife and daughter.

Miss Marjoribanks grew extremely pale

when she saw this unwonted visitor, for
she knew that Mrs Badger would never
come to the manse unless on some serious
errand.

" What news of our poor Andrew ? " asked
Mr Marjoribanks, anxiously.

" There's a warrant oot for his apprehension," replied Mrs Badger, faintly.

" On what charge ? "

" Treason."

Miss Marjoribanks gave an inarticulate
cry, and clasped her hands together.

Mrs Marjoribanks, who was seated in a
low arm-chair, daintily arrayed in a flowered
silk gown, and with a lace cap on her comely
head, leaned forward a little and looked at
her husband, her daughter, and Mrs Badger
in turn.

" Does no one know where he is ? " she
asked, calmly.

Mrs Badger mournfully shook her head.

" He'll no wish to bring his friends into
trouble," she said. " He was aye consider-
ate, puir laddie," and a tear stole down her
furrowed cheek.

" What will be the consequences ? " asked
Mr Marjoribanks, after a long and melancholy pause.

" He'll be outlawed, and killed if he puts
foot on Scottish soil.   That's what the messenger-at-arms told me."

" Oh, that's exaggeration," said Mr Marjoribanks.   " Our laws are not so bad as that."

" God made justice, and man made laws,"
said Mrs Badger, solemnly.   " I wouldna
lippen to the laws."

" Well, Andrew has been very rash and
foolish," said Mrs Marjoribanks, in somewhat
hard, crisp tones.   " I hope it will be a
useful lesson to him."

" Oh, mamma ! " exclaimed Miss Marjoribanks in sorrowful expostulation.

" Poor Andrew ! " murmured the minister,
mournfully.

" This is the result of schismatic courses
in Church and State," remarked Mrs Marjoribanks.

" Maybe that's true, ma'am," said Mrs
Badger, with an indignant sniff.   " But it's
cauld comfort.   However, I must not take

up your time, ma'am. It's taking a liberty
to call, but I couldna help mysel'."

"We are much obliged to you, Mrs Badger," said Mr Marjoribanks. . "Let us know
if anything further occurs. Andrew is a
heavy loss to me — he was my right-hand
man. Such a worthy fellow, and such a
precentor. I wonder whom I shall get to
take his place."

"We'll hae to make melody in our hearts
to the Lord," said Mrs Badger.

Mrs Marjoribanks stood softly patting the
back of one hand with the palm of the
other.

"Oh, I'm gangin', ma'am, I'm gangin',"
said Mrs Badger with alacrity, "and muckle
obliged for Christian sympathy."

Miss Marjoribanks accompanied Mrs Badger to the door.

"We must all pray for him," she said in
a low and tearful voice.

"Very true, miss," said Mrs Badger,
drearily; "but, wae's me, the heavens are
like brass!" She paused for a few minutes,

and then said in an almost inaudible voice, "He fair worshipped you, miss. I could read him like a book. He kenned you was far above him, and he maybe let his modesty wrang him : to be such a bold man, he was unco blate. I suppose naething could hae come o' it. He was puir, very puir—it's a queer warld, miss — a' throughither ! Puir Andrew, he had a big heart. And I was never overly kind to him. That's what vexes me now. I flyted whiles, and glunshed at him, God forgie me !"

It was no slight evidence of Mrs Badger's sympathetic appreciation of Miss Marjoribanks' character that she unbosomed herself so freely.

"Do not reproach yourself, dear Mrs Badger," said the young girl, much moved. "He always spoke so highly of you, and knew your real worth."

"Oh, dinna speak like that," said Mrs Badger, now weeping freely. "I canna stand it — my punishment is greater than I can bear. I dinna wonder that he thocht so much o' you. 'Many daughters have done virtuously, but thou excellest them all.'"

And crushing Miss Marjoribanks' slender fingers in her horny palm, she bade her good-bye, and went away with drooping head and languid gait.

END OF THE FIRST VOLUME.

PRINTED BY WILLIAM BLACKWOOD AND SONS.

POPULAR NOVELS.

EACH COMPLETE IN ONE VOLUME.

THE STORY OF MARGRÉDEL: Being a Fireside History of a Fifeshire Family. By D. STORRAR MELDRUM. Crown 8vo, 6s.

"Is extremely well worth reading, being not only touched by a dramatist's hand, but told in a style which renders it extremely attractive."—*Daily Telegraph.*

TIMAR'S TWO WORLDS. By Maurus Jokai. Authorised Translation by Mrs Hegan Kennard. New Edition. Crown 8vo, 6s.

"'Timar's Two Worlds' may not only be regarded as the author's masterpiece, but as a masterpiece of European literature."—*Athenæum.*

THE CITY OF SUNSHINE. By Alexander Allardyce, Author of 'Earlscourt,' 'Balmoral,' &c. New Edition. Crown 8vo, 6s.

"'The City of Sunshine' is an entrancing story."—*Morning Post.*

MONA MACLEAN, Medical Student. By Graham Travers. Eighth Edition. Crown 8vo, 6s.

"One of the freshest and brightest novels of the time."—*Academy.*

SARACINESCA. By F. Marion Crawford, Author of 'Mr Isaacs,' &c., &c. Sixth Edition. Crown 8vo, 6s.

"Clever, stirring, interesting."—*Spectator.*

THE MAID OF SKER. By R. D. Blackmore, Author of 'Lorna Doone,' &c. New Edition. Crown 8vo, 6s.

"A genuine success, one of the few good novels that have been written for many years."—*Spectator.*

SINGULARLY DELUDED. By Sarah Grand, Author of 'The Heavenly Twins,' 'Ideala,' &c. Crown 8vo, 6s.

"Sensations follow each other in this book with the rapidity of revolver shots."—*Daily Chronicle.*

A DOMESTIC EXPERIMENT. By the Same Author. Crown 8vo, 6s.

"Cleverly and gracefully written."—*Scotsman.*

WILLIAM BLACKWOOD & SONS, Edinburgh and London.

www.ingramcontent.com/pod-product-compliance
Lightning Source LLC
Chambersburg PA
CBHW060600030726
47498CB00005B/1470